THE TRIALS OF YOUNG

David Kirk

BY

DAVID A. PETERSON

ISBN: 978-1-961879-24-9 (sc)
978-1-961879-25-6 (e)

Publishing rev. date: 09/24/2023

AUTHOR CABIN

THE PLACE FOR YOUR STORY

THE TRIALS OF YOUNG

David Kirk

Contents

CHAPTER 1

THE SECRET OF LIEUTENANT GONZALEZ

"Oh God do I love looking at this," said Admiral Richardson out loud to himself in his empty office, "not another soul here and I'm loving it." He ran his right-hand fingers gently along that rough, brown, thin, long, clove cigarette. A rare moment indeed, enhanced with an equally rare smoke, a Krakatoa Kretek, from the mid 1900's. The Admiral thought his dad could not have done any better. A banned smoke of its time but a treasured family secret, and that huge cooler my dad had in his storage shed where the Krakatoa's were stored, kept agelessly. A fantastic hidden secret in his dad's vineyard located in California's Sonoma County.

Bringing that Kretek up to his soft ruddy lips, holding that smoke firmly in the finders of his right hand he carefully lit this beauty, holding it ever so gently.

Admiral Richardson relaxed as he thoroughly appreciated his first long, relaxing inhale while watching the reflection of his chest on his office picture-window, "Now that shows too much truth". He loved these rare quiet moments as he cherished that view from his desk, especially right now with that red-golden glow setting Sun, wrapping softly around the Golden Gate Bridge, like loving arms hugging a great friend.

Admiral Richardson's 'Star Fleet Academy Office' was a second home to him. As he savored this rare moment, he looked again at his reflection in the office window, observing his muscle-barreled chest, and his growing, round, and now slightly bulging stomach, which he blamed entirely on his wife Marian's excellent home baking. As he thought about this, he almost drooled, picturing her totally evil but delicious blueberry and cherry pies. He patted his stomach and started to laugh, knowing that his was not due to his lack of working-out lately. "Damn" the Admiral stated out-loud with the office echoing, that jelly-belly dance could become embarrassing.

The Admiral was suddenly startled by an incredibly loud knocking on his closed office door which sent him into a short shocking jump. "Wow", said the Admiral," that damned near scared me."

That just goes to prove that me jumping hurdles in track will never be my thing. Damn, there goes that knocking again. I'm tempted to yell "incoming" like out of an old-World War II movie, and damn, there we go again with another loud, strong knocking on my door.

"All right, all right, quite pounding on my damned door and come in!" stated the Admiral in a loud commanding voice, giving him a quick reminder of his field training days. How I did enjoy those days, watching those new recruits shake in fear as I yelled at them to stand at attention and then ordering them to do fifty pushups for being such losers.

Admiral Richardson turned towards the front of his responsibility, while at the same time, breathing in deeply, savoring this last long draw of his Krakatoa. As the door was opening the Admiral put out his Krakatoa, returning what remained into its container, which he then quickly slipped into his desk cooler. His saving space for quiet reclusive moments.

"Oh, it's you Jose, you have definitely impressed me with this entry, but I don't like it, not one damned bit. Here I am cherishing a moment of isolation in my rarely empty office. I had truly escaped from responsibility for a moment."

As the Admiral stood behind his desk, he took a strong look at a brown leather case that Lieutenant Gonzalez was carrying. There was a chain coming from the Lieutenants left wrist to the handle of the briefcase.

Lt. Gonzales, the Admirals personal secretary, stumbled as he was approaching the Admirals desk. The Lieutenant swung his stiff left leg forward. He had been injured in a defensive action a few years ago in Star Fleet. Word had it that Jose had an upcoming date at the Academy Hospital for a genetically cloned leg replacement.

Jose had been shaken by the unexpected strength of the Admirals rough challenge as he was looking back over his left shoulder at the two security guards standing, armed and at attention, just outside the door.

The Admiral stood with hands on his hips with an expression of total disgust, looking at his lieutenant and those two guards. The Admirals shoulders jumped as his office door shut with a great force which even sent a few papers flying off the top of his desk. "Well, you may stumble a little bit there Jose but even from a distance you can upset my desk. Quite the talent you have their Lieutenant."

In this chaotic moment Jose saluted the Admiral which was totally out of the ordinary between them.

Admiral Richardson saluted back to his secretary, Lieutenant Gonzalez. The Admiral had a harsh, puzzled look on his face as he looked at Jose. The Admiral Richardson forcefully stated to Jose, "Lieutenant, tell me, what in the hell are guards doing outside my door! What could my fantastic personal secretary possibly have done to deserve such an escort back to my office," voiced the Admiral, just short of a loud field command yell. Then looking at Lieutenant Gonzalez, the Admiral started to chuckle and said, "it has been a long time since I have seen that look dragging on your face, Lieutenant. And I do mean the look on your face, not your walk, Lieutenant," said the Admiral directly into Jose's eyes.

The atmosphere in the office suddenly lightened up, welcomed by both officers. The Admiral and the Lieutenant were now breathing slower and smiling at each other, both letting go somewhat of this stressful moment.

"Admiral replied to Lieutenant Gonzalez with an easier, softer voice, "wait until my husband Greg hears what you said."

Both the Lieutenant and the Admiral were laughing now.

"Whew," stated the Admiral, "we have never started a day out like this, but I guess it is fair to say that 'shit happens' Lieutenant. Let's not do it again, ok?" "I agree Sir," replied the Lieutenant.

"I have never walked into something like this Lieutenant and once is just too damn much," stated the Admiral. "I think Lieutenant that before you explain what is going on here, and I must say that my intuition tells me that this is going to be a long evening and an evening with you Jose.

So, how about extending this strange time and order a tall pot of espresso and something to eat. I was just thinking, how about four of those veggie burgers you like so much and a double order of your other favorites, Venusian Fries.

What say you Lieutenant?"

"Sounds great Admiral. And yes, we will be here for a while Sir, alone and together," replied Lieutenant Gonzalez with a light chuckle.

Lightheartedly Admiral Richardson said, "I bet you informed my wife, Betty, and your husband, Greg, long before the beginning of this damned mess, right Lieutenant?"

"Why of course, Sir," replied Lieutenant Gonzalez, "Greg was loving and compassionate when I told him I would most likely not be home for another day or two and that I was spending that time, alone, and with you Sir. Greg laughingly said that we should enjoy our time together.

But, on the other hand, what your wife said about that is another story, Sir."

"I guess, Lieutenant, from what you say, you and Greg won't be out dancing this evening, although I would bet that you drag a little in a three step, let alone line- dancing." Welcomed laughter bounced around the office.

CHAPTER 2

AN EXPLANATION

A chill came across Jose's neck as he was looking at the Admirals facial expression. The mood in the office changed to a somber, heavy silence. Lieutenant Jose thought for a moment that secrecy didn't seem like such a big deal when he initially joined Star Fleet. The obligation of secrecy seemed more like an article in Star Fleet Regulations than any possible real responsibility, especially one that he ended up carrying.

Hopefully he would be freed now, drop the anchor and cut its chain. When Jose was offered and accepted this responsibility, he had no idea how this would weigh him down into a private agony which had become part of his everyday life and as he quietly thought, a never-ending pain in the ass. Jose thought this would all be so much easier after he was informed that Captain Kirk and Dr. Carol Marcus both carried the same secret, but it never got any lighter. Tonight, hopefully, sharing this with Admiral Richardson would free him from this endless, dark experience where he occasionally felt as if he was in a private prison that no one else could see nor help him escape.

Many years ago, at the start of all this, he thought these restless, sleepless nights were just natural from his duty with the Admiral, but slowly he began to see it differently. On many of those sleepless nights at home, he would quietly slip out of bed as if he were headed to the bathroom. Then he would carefully slip down to their library, and carefully, quietly, shut the library door. While sitting at the desk he shed a few quiet tears while grabbing a couple of tissues from the tissue box on the desk. But Jose was not as quiet as he thought which he soon found out.

One evening, suddenly, Greg walked in on him in their library, catching Jose bent over at the desk in muffled tears. Greg's love showed deeply the first time that he walked in on Jose as Greg immediately asked Jose if he had done something to hurt Jose and Greg began to shed tears like a small river. Jose said, no, it's about work, and he couldn't discuss it, I am so sorry Greg."

Later that evening Jose said to Greg, "when I'm cold to my bones in these moments, and I think of you Greg it is only your love that warms me."

When these times repeated themselves, Greg would find Jose again tearfully in their library and Greg would say, "come on Jose, let's go to bed and let me hold you, just hold you. Jose thought numerous times that Greg was truly his lifeguard, his needed personal time of comfort and peace. Jose chuckled one time which relieved Greg's heavy face, saying to him, "you're' my "May West"[1] Greg". Jose felt so blessed with his husband Greg that he thought, "wife, husband, what is a word when you're in love".

Jose always felt safe and relaxed in their bedroom. He loved the bedroom glass walls. Often Jose would open the glass sliding doors and go out into that walled garden, enjoying his many flowers and that bench between the three Redwood trees. He loved to sit on that bench, listening to all those birds who relished the birdbaths and feeders. He spoiled them rotten, and they loved it. Often, one or more of the neighborhood cats would come over to him on the bench, lay across his lap while waiting for Jose to brush their hair backwards which they

---

[1] "May West" in 1931 the nickname for the inflatable life preserver, named after actress May West due to her being 'buxom' (having large breasts)

loved, dearly purring in response while their legs would go stiff, and their claws would extend.

Occasionally the cats would be waiting for him in their guest houses, small Victorian houses that Jose placed along the back wall behind the Redwood trees.

Looking at the Admirals face, Jose immediately returned to the present. And now it was time to follow through with his orders, to share his responsibility with his Admiral. Jose felt as though he was preparing an impossible answer to a crazy word puzzle.

Captain Kirk, Jose thought quietly to himself, I need you now. If you can hear me in your spirit, comfort me please, Captain Kirk, please.

Okay, thanks, a break at last thought Lt. Gonzalez to himself as there was a light knock on the door which had to be their food order.

"Great," said the Admiral, "I really need that espresso right now. And something to eat. I bet you're ready Lieutenant for some espresso and something to eat. I will get the cart since security will not allow any service to enter."

As the Admiral went to retrieve the cart, he couldn't help but take notice of the lady delivering the food cart. She reminded the Admiral of his daughter, JoeLynn. Presently, JoyLynn who was off leading the restructuring of Star-Base 15. The Admiral smiled as he thought about JoeLynn winning those Lego structural design challenges in her elementary and high-school years at the Star-Fleet Student Academy.

"Thank you" stated the Admiral as he took the food cart from the server and pulled it into the office. As soon as he got that cart in the office, security shut that Door, a little too hard. The Admiral turned sharply and flipped his middle finger toward the door as he felt intentionally locked-out against the world.

The Admiral wheeled the cart over to the serving table near his desk, and then hit the window security dimming switch on the corner of the desk as if he were smashing a bug. His office window went immediately into a reflective security, blocking visibility in or out, which he knew was required by this security level.

"Now Lieutenant, let's see. The first thing we better do is get that handcuff off your wrist and then let's get that valise opened, ok?" stated the Admiral.

"I'm for that. The key will be in the office mail on your desk, sir," quietly replied to the Lieutenant.

The Admiral found the envelope, opened it and showed the key to Jose, then unlocked the cuff on Jose's left wrist.

Lieutenant Gonzalez said to the Admiral, "to open this nightmare for the evening, Sir, we both have to place our right hand, at the same time, on your desks security-file reader, and then it will open. One, two, three", strongly voiced Lieutenant Gonzalez, then he and the Admiral placed the palms of their right hands on the desk security-file reader, and the immediately the mechanism released the seal on the valise with a loud 'thump'.

"Wow, this is always such a strange process when I have to do it, Lieutenant," said Admiral Richardson, "and now that we have this accomplished, I am going to go around to my chair after I grab my cup of espresso, and sit for a moments rest, quietly. It is a good thing I didn't have that espresso in my other hand when we did this as I would have thrown my espresso across the room with that 'thump'. That thing never is gentle when it opens something, always an unexpected shocker to me." Admiral Richardson filled an espresso cup for himself and one for his Lieutenant, handing Jose his as he walked around to his side of his desk in a little heavier gate than usual. If one looked at the Admirals face as he sat down in his chair you would see a tight frown from which one might think he was preparing to discipline his Lieutenant.

Silence filled the moment as they both sipped their espressos. The Admiral thought this might be his last relaxing moment for such a long time this evening, but difficult to truly accept. He was thinking that someone really knows how to make espresso, perhaps just for me, and that thought brought a relaxing smile to his face.

After a good five minutes of quiet, the Admiral said, "Lieutenant, perhaps you can tell me the story behind this drama before you open that valise and let me know what is hidden so deep that you seem to enjoy the darkness. I am wondering how you of all people were assigned such a security clearance.

I can't believe you have never mentioned this to me, Jose.

Ok Jose, come on now, speak up!"

"Sir," said Lieutenant Gonzalez, "as we move along into this revelation, I believe it will all become clear."

"Well, I accept that Lieutenant. So, get on with my good man!" replied the Admiral.

Lieutenant Gonzalez replied, "Ok Sir, here we go. This will be a lot to bite into but together we will get through it. To begin with Sir, tomorrow morning, Sunday, a new ambassador will be arriving right here, at your landing deck, Sir."

"At my landing deck, now that is strange. Well, this must be damned important as I have no such information on my calendar or in any of my office mail. And I never received a call which I would expect on anything like this, especially on such short notice. So, is there an issue with this ambassador? Perhaps he is married and likes every woman he can get his hands on? This is just strange, very strange indeed Lieutenant," replied the Admiral.

"I wish it were that simple, I wish it truly were, Sir" replied the Lieutenant.

"Ok, ok then Jose, I need another espresso and a burger, with the fries. Then my Lieutenant, I will sit down and shut up, which is truly amazing to hear from me, right Lieutenant?"

"Right Admiral, definitely." Jose got up and grabbed two bottles of water from the sidebar while the Admiral got two espressos. Jose got himself a burger and a set of his favorite Venusian Fries.

As Jose opened the case the entry office door security system automatically set itself, dead bolting the security locks.

Jose reflected to himself that now after a very long time he could dump his burden. I have no doubt that without Greg I could never had carried this weight, not at all. Now I understand a cross, holy shit!

"Ok Lieutenant, what is this ambassadors name and how can he be so damned important. Besides, believe it or not, I'm ready to listen. On nice, you got us both a bottle of water." The Admiral shook his head as he looked at the open file upon Jose's lap. Then he looked Jose directly in his eyes as he leaned back in his chair and raised his espresso in a slow appreciative salute to Jose.

Jose returned the salute, saying, "Admiral, his full name is Ambassador ShaNeenSed, and ShaNeenSed is one long word as we say it. But, Admiral, ShaNeenSed is by their language, three words and each having its first letter capitalized. Here Sir, this will make more sense if I use our projector. Seeing much of this information will give it more clarity.

Divulging this history to you, Sir will lead us on into a very long night which I believe will go deep into the morning, Sir. And as we get into this history it will slowly be revealed how I was assigned this security level. Tomorrow the ambassador will arrive as I already stated.

His arrival has already been granted clearance through the United Federation of Planets, and from the President herself. The ambassador is arriving here at your office, as Sir, you have been designated as the official officer to receive the Ambassador."

"Lieutenant that's it? I welcome this mysterious ambassador that no one has any information on. This is amazing Jose, simply amazing. So why this secrecy. Is this ambassador some type of unpopular asshole? Or is he hiding something," asked the Admiral?

"He is a good man Admiral. The Ambassador's name is one long word with three capital letters as I said before. Regardless of how it looks in that projection Sir, in English his name is pronounced Sha Neen Said. The closest English spelling is as you see it projected. In reading their language, the capital letters are extremely important. Sir, we will follow their writing style, but we won't get into their language. We best leave that for another day."

"Maybe we can just set that aside and leave it there. I think I'm good in English and that's enough for me right now," stated Admiral Richardson.

"No problem, Sir. I have seen their writing which I call a script as in an art form," replied Lieutenant Gonzalez. "Here we go. The Ambassador's name is a title and name composed of three separate words. Oddly, they read from the present to the past. What I mean by that is that 'Sha' means 'ambassador'. We have translated 'Neen' as accurately as we can, and it means 'mental health therapist'. And finally, 'Sed' is the Ambassador's family name. Like mine, Gonzalez, or yours Sir, Richardson.' 'Sed' being the family name, it is placed last as I'm pointing out, behind any title or rank in the order of its achievement, being that the first title, the oldest, is first placed directly in front of the family name. This is considered one word, even after additions in front of the family name. Admiral, this all begins, believe it or not, with Star Fleet Captain Kirk's son, David Marcus."

"Lieutenant, you have to be kidding me, but that look on your face tells me you're very damned serious. So, carry on Lieutenant, carry on."

"Quite so Admiral, quite so." The Lieutenant stood up and started walking a little in front of the desk as he continued, "I have a hidden story to tell you of David Marcus which is a great part of this Security File. With the co-operation of both Admiral Kirk and Dr. Carol Marcus, this history has only been shared by those committed to its security. Even a few Klingons and Romulans are part of this story and those in the know, agree with the security."

The Admiral interrupted Jose, "So you're stating Jose that the Klingons and Romulans are involved also, wow. I believe they would keep any secret, but I am astounded those humans have kept this secret. Sorry for interrupting Lieutenant, please carry on," said the Admiral.

"I think it is common knowledge today, Sir, that David Marcus did not know for many, many years, that Admiral Kirk was his father. His mother, Dr. Carol Marcus, in all the years of raising David only mentioned Admiral Kirk as an old, old friend. It is public record that David Marcus earned his Doctoral Degree at 23 and worked with his mother before and after acquiring his degree in Astrophysics.

It is known now that shortly after David turned 16, he had found the same love his mother had for "terraforming"[2] a planet.

No doubt that due to his mother's influence and some under the-table action by then Captain Kirk. David was assigned as an assistant in that ships Astrophysics Department as he wanted to be in the exploration of new systems and planets. The ship officially was registered as the NCC 21167, 'the USS Baikonur", which was a Star Fleet Miranda class vessel. There exists no public documentation on this ship or any printed record of its staff or mission. I will divulge this record as I move along in this story, Sir.

We do know that David boarded this ship at our Earth Docking Station, right next to, of all ships, the Enterprise, which was then under the command of Captain Kirk."

Admiral Richardson interjected, "Oh, totally an accident I'm sure Lieutenant. From what I understand, David was absent from his classes for at least two years. And what amazes me is that he never fell behind in his studies during his travels. I was told one night that David had moved well ahead of his class schedule and built his doctoral foundation while being absent from classes. I can't wait to hear more but first let's refill our espresso and grab anything else you want Jose.

---

[2] "Terraforming" - Modifying environment of planet or moon to make it habitable for life.

The way you're pacing around perhaps a bottle of water instead of any coffee. What say you Lieutenant?" said the Admiral.

"Sir, first I need to use the bathroom, and then I definitely need another espresso. And just maybe a burger on the desk, Sir."

Jose looked in the bathroom mirror, considering his reflection he slid into some cherished relaxing thoughts. He thought that he would love driving home right now instead of going through this, even if it was the usual congested rush hour traffic.

In this uncomfortable moment, Jose suddenly realized how much he truly loved his husband, Greg. Greg Aloysius, what a timely last name, meaning 'famous battle'.

Jose's husband, Greg, always met him at the front door as he arrived home, with a welcoming hug and a loving kiss. As Jose entered their log home, well, more of a lodge in style really, Greg would hand Jose his favorite drink after a day's work, a dry martini-up.

Greg then would turn about and be off into his kitchen. Jose felt very blessed to be married to a chef and one who teaches on the net.

Then with ease Joe sat down his martini on the entry table, off with his boots, pick up his drink, and then down into their sunken living room and gently relaxed into his favorite vibrational lounge chair. That's what I need right now, responsibility turned off and off my feet, oh yeah.

Jose noticed, thankfully, that the Admiral had placed his espresso and a burger with Venusian Fries on his side of the desk. Obviously, the Admiral had used his personal code to over-ride the security black-out of the office window which is just what Jose liked.

"This is a hell of a lot better don't you think Jose", stated the admiral while looking through the dim view of the office window. "Lieutenant let's get on with it," said the Admiral as he turned away from the window, facing Jose as he pulled out his desk chair.

"We're well on our way, Sir, and now into the unbelievable as I used to think of it. And thank you Sir for partially clearing the window as I was beginning to feel somewhat claustrophobic. I can get on with this now," stated the Lieutenant.

"Lieutenant forgive me for interrupting you, but I was wondering if you have a photo of this ShaNeenSed?"

"No Sir. To my knowledge only David Marcus has meet ShaNeenSed and the two developed quite a friendship. David is also the only individual in 'the United Federation" and "Star Fleet" that has been on ShaNeenSed's home planet. Over time David was introduced to the culture and history of ShaNeenSed's home planet, whose name is BathKohl.

Most of the information we have acquired was discovered shortly after David's unfortunate death.

Madam President of the "United Federation of Planets" has spent some time in meetings and negotiation with ShaNeenSed from the Paris Headquarters.

The communication was of the utmost secrecy as requested by an individual or group that is equal, we believe, to the elected officials of our Federation. I was beginning to think that this was a test of my security precautions, to see if I would follow protocol. But now I see this is a night I would never dream of or want to for that matter. Thank you for your patience and believe me, you have my undivided attention Lieutenant."

"Sir, I am going to begin with a quote that has helped to keep me settled, somewhat, while holding this secret.

"The greatest danger facing us is an irrational fear of the unknown. But there's no such thing as the unknown – only things temporarily hidden, temporarily not understood."[3]

---

[3] "The Autobiography of James T. Kirk" by Memory Alpha Historian and Editor David A. Goodman

Now Sir, I will start the David Marcus when he was injured while attending his studies at the Mars "Sojourner Ranch" at only 16 years old. David no sooner graduated from our Star Fleet High School after two years that he was immediately accepted at Sojourner for his goal to achieve a Ph.D. in Astrophysics. He wanted to work with his mother in astrophysics, so this was a real win for him.

CHAPTER 3

DAVID MARCUS – A STUDENT AT THE DAYSTROM INSTITUTE

David was waking-up in the Intensive Care Recovery Unit at the Sojourner Ranch Hospital, located in the Utopia Planitia on the planet Mars.

While sitting up in his hospital bed a call came in from his mother which utterly thrilled David. David touched his communicator that was attached to the front of his hospital gown. "Wow, hi Mom. I am so glad to hear from you. I'm looking around here and wondering what ever happened that I appear to be in a hospital ward. Do you know what's going on mother?"

"Well David, first I will say that I believe your memory will be returning soon. I can tell you what I know, and I expect that this will help you find your memory again. I bet it looks like a hospital, right David?" replied David's Mother, Dr. Carol Marcus.

Yes mother, but I feel like I'm in a sick, sick dream," replied David looking at his mother on the viewing screen with a frown on his face.

"David, you're in the Intensive Care Unit at the Sojourner Hospital on Mars. I will start with a few questions that hopefully will help you remember why and how you got here in this hospital unit. Let's backup a little David and I will start with the fact that you were accepted at the Daystrom University on Mars in your favorite area of study, astrophysics. And you have recently applied to the Astrophysics Department on the USS Baikonur. That mission will be its first mission, one of exploration. Do you remember anything about that David?" asked David's Mother.

"What I remember right now Mother, is that I was feeling isolated, maybe even claustrophobic and shut-in at the University, shortly after I arrived. I know this was my first time on my own away from Earth. I figured even though I might feel isolated on a ship especially with probably a year on my first journey that I would be alright because of my studies. With any luck I will be beaming down onto a few new discovered planets and that would make it all worthwhile, for sure!

Mother, continuing my studies on the Baikonur and eventually being an assistant in your terraforming research with you would be the greatest personal freedom I have had in a long, long time.

There is no way I could beat being on a research vessel and studying Astrophysics, following in your path mother and as I say, "going where I have never been before".

"That is just great David, just great."

"I do have a difficult question for you mother, if you don't mind," said David with a little apprehension in his voice.

"Ok David, I'm all ears."

"Mother I wish that I could get a call from my dad, whoever he is. I know you have never discussed this with me but now I could use an answer," David said while looking directly into his mother's eyes on the visual communication monitor. "I'm sorry David, but (with a small pause and a little stuttering) I am just not sure who your dad really is. Please forgive me David, but I just can't talk about this right now," replied David's mother.

"That does tick me a little, but ok Mother. But I will come back to this at another time."

"David, someday I will be okay with talking about this, but not right now David, I want to concentrate on you and what happened to you. I have had a few sessions on screen with your doctor, whose name is Dr. Bayshare. Dr. Bayshare called me shortly after your surgery and gave me all the pertinent information. If you like we can discuss this later."

"Mother, hopefully you won't mind but I am definitely ready to hear what happened to me right now, okay?"

"Okay David, I can continue on with this. Anything else first?"

"Yes Mother, I think so. I have a few experiences to share which made me very uncomfortable in the past few days."

"Go ahead David, I'm all ears. Do you want a close-up on the screen of one of my ears?" replied Dr. Marcus with some light chuckling.

"I think I can pass on that mother, thanks for the offer though", said David with a definite smile on his face and a wink of his left eye. Got ya" said David with a definite chuckle. So, mother, one night I woke up from a terrible nightmare. In that nightmare I was sitting in a plain old wooden rocking-chair without even a pillow, and no pillow would certainly be unusual for me. Odd though, I just didn't care if I had a pillow or not. In that dream I was dredging up ways to maintain my isolation even though it made me uncomfortable. The walls were grey, and I could see my reflection on the walls. And my brown eyes were now grey, and of all things, my hair had been cut off and my head shined. After waking up I figured that dream had to be a side effect from one of my meds. And then in another dream I thought I couldn't walk. I was seeing myself on a road that had no direction that I could see, and the road signs had nothing on them, they were totally blank. I was holding a compass and it had no direction letters on its face. I can say these dreams seemed more like an old slide show," said David as he was wiping away a few tears on his face. David noticed his heart beginning to jump on the medical monitor, so he took a few deep relaxing breaths. "Mom, If I remember a little of Doctor Bayshare, I remember him saying that I had a spinal block during the surgery. After waking up from the surgery I thought I had somehow been paralyzed from my waist down. I was dumbfounded with shock. It wasn't soon enough to me when I was finally told about the spinal block and that feeling, and the full use of my legs would return. I was so relieved to hear that in a moment I started to heavily cry. I shed so many tears that my nurse brought me a fresh gown.

I only remember one nurse in the unit right now and if I remember right her name is Carolyn. There may be others, but Carolyn is the only one I remember right now.

Mom, so where are you right now? Are you coming to visit as I would really like to spend some time with you? It's been a few years since we have spent any time together."

"I'm so sorry David but there is no way I can come to visit at all due to my work." "So, Mom, what you're you are doing that you can't visit me at all?"

"David, I cannot talk about my project, but I did hear on the rumor line that you're studying terraforming, but you know how rumors are David," replied David's Mother with a wide smile on her face.

"Got it mother, thanks. Just a second mom, someone's at the door."

"Oh wow, hello Dr. Bayshare, amazing, I remember your name. I'm thrilled I recognized you. Good timing Dr. Bayshare, my mother is on the visual screen and was getting ready to tell me what happened," said David.

"This is great David, just great. I can spend some time with both of you and tell you both exactly what I know. Dr. Marcus, you are welcomed to remain in communication" stated Dr. Bayshare, bringing an immediate reply from Dr. Marcus, "thank you Doctor Bayshare, I would really appreciate you taking this on right now."

Dr. Bayshare pulled a large reclining chair over to David's bedside and sat down, enjoying the chair as he became relaxed.

"If it's okay with you Dr. Marcus, we can change your communication from this flat communicator to a holographic projection of yourself."

"That's a super choice. Let's do it Doctor," replied Dr. Marcus.

Dr. Bayshare crossed his legs as he looked upon the holographic image of Dr. Marcus and he thought how amazingly beautiful this woman is. Imagine, she is tops in astrophysics, and then wow, such a beautiful woman. And her brown eyes are simply beautiful, they just seem to sparkle. This woman is absolutely gorgeous. Interesting, her hair is straight and David's curly. Her figure, why she looks more like a model to me, even in that white research robe she has on. I would love to date this woman. Her skin is so white and clear looking. I know I am a good swimmer, but swimming with her, and doing 'the breaststroke'. Hmmm, I love my evil thoughts. Guess I better get myself back together and pay attention.

"Dr. Bayshare, you seem to be a little off-center right now. Are you okay?" asked Dr. Marcus.

"Oh, I'm fine Dr. Marcus. Excuse me but your hologram appears so real to me that I was caught off guard for a moment," replied Dr. Bayshare with a little startle in his voice and a red-blushed face.

"That's alright Doctor, but I do have to return to my lab shortly so why don't I just listen to both of you and grab a chair as I need to sit down. Please carry-on Doctor." The image of Dr. Marcus faded out and quickly returned as she could be seen dragging a chair and sat down near Dr. Bayshare, close to the head of David's bed.

Dr. Bayshare sat up straight and blushed in his face again as Dr. Marcus sat next to him while focusing on David saying, "David, to my understanding you arrived early for your classes at our 'Daystrom Institute of Technology' for studies in Astrophysics, the same field as your mother's, if I am correct David."

"Oh yes, I do remember my arrival and meeting up with other students but while a little foggy right now it is getting clearer as I sit here," said David as he was pulling the bedtable over for a needed drink of water.

Dr. Bayshare continued on saying, "David, apparently you had met and became close to a fellow student, Marian LaForge. At some time, you and Marian LaForge decided to visit together, the historic site of the Mars Rover "Curiosity" Historic Trail where the first organic molecules were discovered at the Mars 'Gale Crater' in 2018."

As Miss LaForge and yourself approached that history plaque on the trail there was a large explosion. Luckily there was several security cameras which fed to the security offices at the Utopia Planitia Fleet Yards. The security office saw the event and immediately dispatched a full medical response. Being part of that response team, I was utterly shocked as the catastrophe was so tragic and strange, especially when so many others have walked that path long before you two," said Dr. Bayshare.

Then David sat straight up in his bed, while trembling a little and shedding a few tears, asked, "Dr. Bayshare, how is Marian. She is the first girl I have every felt attracted to and I think we were getting closer to each other since that first day we meet at the University."

Dr. Bayshare suddenly cleared his throat, stating, "I'm sorry David, there is no easy way to tell you this. I pronounced Marian dead only a few minutes after my arrival in the blast area."

David broke down into loud tears upon hearing of Marian' s death.

Dr. Marcus reached out to David but her holographic form kept fracturing while she said, "I'm so sorry David. I just wish I could hold you right now. David, I know you're going to be alright."

"Thank you, mother. I have never felt like this before. Wow, I'm recalling that shortly after arriving at the historical trail, a loose stick was lying on the ground and Marian picked it up, took a swing with it, and fell to the ground. We were laughing as we both forgot the light gravity and stiffness of our space suits.

I asked her why she did that and Marian told me she had started playing in a resurrected sport back on Earth shortly before coming here, called Ice Hockey. She said this women's team was part of the sport comeback, called the 'Pittsburgh Penguins'.

Dr. Marcus's projection showed her moving back to her office chair while slightly dabbing her own eyes with a hanky.

After a few minutes of quiet in the room, Dr. Marcus turned towards Dr. Bayshare, asking him, "Doctor, is it known what happened to create this nightmare?"

"Yes Dr. Marcus. I'm amazed we figured it out as everyone working on the investigation was utterly dumbfounded. It appears from our research that sometime in October of 2158 in the Earth-Romulan War there was a successful attack by the Romulans, targeting the Utopia Planitia Shipyards. The Romulans had placed many land mine devices in several areas, and it was an old land mine device which through time ended directly under the walking trail which David and Marian were walking on.

David, when you and Marian approached the historical information sign on the location of Curiosity's discovery it appears that the vibrations from your walking set the mine off.

I can add that following this disaster, we sent a communication to Romulus and no answer has ever been received from Romulus," explained Dr. Bayshare.

"Not even an apology?" asked David with disgust sounding in his voice.

"No apology ever arrived David. And I don't think we will every receive an apology or any communication from Romulus on this incident, especially since it was a war issue," said Dr. Bayshare.

CHAPTER 4

DAVID'S INTRODUCTION TO PLANET "BATHKOHL"

David was absolutely thrilled while looking out of a shuttle-pod[4] window near his seat as they were approaching Earth Station McKinley. Earth Station McKinley was in synchronous orbit above the Earth over San Francisco, California.

David could see the USS Enterprise docked alongside the USS Baikonur. He was surprised at the size of the Enterprise next to the Baikonur. David was getting excited as he looked at his future home and his future classroom, the USS Baikonur, for at least the next 12 months.

David had set a goal of only 'A's or whatever is equal to an 'A' in his class work. He wanted to do this as his private way of honoring his first love, Marian LaForge. David was thinking that growing up is so damned difficult at times and so painful at times. The shuttle-pod was nearing its docking to the Earth Station McKinley as he took another look of amazement at the USS Enterprise. He thought it would be so great if only he could have meant his mom's friend, Captain Kirk of the Enterprise while here. But he knew that there was no way that could happen this time.

---

4 Shuttle-pod NC-05

An announcement came through the speakers, "Please return to your seats and put on your seat-belts as we will be docking shortly. Please remain in your seats until our door opens to the station. At the door you will be welcomed by an escort and shown to the reception station. Thank you." The wait seemed like forever to David, but it was only a few minutes after docking that the door to Station McKinley opened. While David was getting from his seat, he took note of the beautiful lady who greeted everyone, "Welcome to Earth Station McKinley. I'm your welcome stewardess, Ms. Jacobs. If you will please follow me, we will first go to the check-in station and process each of you to your respective destinations. Any questions will be answered at the station."

After David checked in, he was asked to wait for a few minutes until his escort arrived from the USS Baikonur.

"I am Lieutenant Longreen and I assume you are David Marcus, right?" "Yes I am."

"David, even though you're a civilian it is appropriate while a shipmate on the Baikonur to greet all officers as 'Sir', unless they say otherwise."

"Yes Sir, I will do my best. Thank you, Lieutenant."

Walking behind Lieutenant Longreen, David was intrigued as he recognized some of the ship from his studies in "The Star-Fleet General Ship Plans Manual". Unknown to David, his studies of the various fleet vessels would one day save his life.

The Baikonur seemed tighter in many areas then David expected, but David was very grateful to be on its staff and he felt extremely gifted as a student on this ship. He thought while he had been okay with the small areas in the Daystrom Institute, here he felt a new freedom and surprisingly, relaxed.

Mr. Marcus, or David if that is alright with you," said Lieutenant Longreen.

"No problem, Sir, thanks. I usually just go by my first name."

"David, I will show you to your compartment and believe me, you're quite lucky on this trip. Usually, you would be housed in the crew's quarters on Deck Four, but you have been assigned to the VIP quarters on Deck Five. And that's great for you David as your located directly above the Astrophysics Lab. That Lab was moved to the front hull area some time ago. Here we are David, and this is your card key for your door entry. David swiped the card in front of the reader and the door opened with a quiet hiss.

"David your luggage will be along shortly, and I will give you an hour to unpack before I return to show you around the ship. I think tonight you will meet the entire Astrophysics Department staff at dinner."

David had no sense of time while the USS Baikonur was exploring in uncharted space. He had never felt so good in any of his past studies as he felt with his work here on the Baikonur. David loved his studies and class assignments in the lab, along with his unexpected co-assignment in Stellar Cartography. He figured he was really taking baby steps into his own unknown.

As pre-planned, the Baikonur was on its first explorative assignment to the outer boundaries of the Milky Way Galaxy's 'Alpha Quadrant'. As the Baikonur reached the Alpha Quadrant the ship came to a complete stop. The stop was at the request of the Astrophysics Department which had just detected a strange but steady signal. This signal didn't match any known language in their Computer Knowledge Banks, nor could that computer system combine any known language to translate this new language. Their first choice was to find its source and gather more information so hopefully they would gather a translation of the language. The staff had no doubt this was a discovery of a new language of unknown origin, a new unknown planet and a very intelligent new species. The question unanswered that the research staff had for each other was when they find this new species, then what? A question filled with some hope, doubt, and little fear.

The Captain of the USS Baikonur, Captain Malinda Benson, came to a decision that while the ship was stopped for the Astrophysics work, she would let the crew take a needed break. Captain Benson announced the off-duty time for most of the crew on this ship's intercom. The captain could hear a response of strong applause, sporty yelling, and 'thank you', all echoing around the corridors of the ship.

Some of the crew retired to their quarters, some to the holo-deck, and others to games, music, and dance, and others, simply lounging around. And as one of the crew members were heard to say, "time for some welcomed sin out of wedlock."

Security was also allowed to cut their usual duty staff in half for the time being as approved by Captain Benson.

Security on the main deck was enjoying good coffee and sweets while on duty, with the pleasure of unimportant conversation.

On the main-deck, a security staff member was on duty, and while leaning on the visual security board hadn't noticed he had accidentally hit the warning sound-off button which turned off the entire ships warning system.

The ships computerized security system had a level of independence designed to over-ride any system-muting when that system detected the approach of a non – Federation vessel which automatically turned on the defensive shields and turn on the red alert level[5] throughout the ship.

The red alerts status warning went loud and wide throughout the ship, strongly startling each crew member. Each crew member moved to their assigned duty station, awaiting further orders from their Captain.

Captain Benson was at her duty station on the bridge and immediately called for her Chief Security Officer, Lieutenant Carson, asking why the ships shields were up and the alarm sounding.

---

[5] "Red Alert Level" - Condition invoked during actual states of emergency

Lieutenant Carson said "that the automated security system recognized that ship as a Miranda Class vessel but there are no such Federation ships, other than ours Sir, in this Quadrant. That undoubtedly set off the defensive system, Captain." Captain Benson facing Lieutenant Carson in a strong firm voice said, "as with our mission classification I certainly would have been notified as to any other mission in this quadrant. It is possible that our defensive mode might be seen as an aggressive act by that ship. I don't believe suspicion is enough to maintain a defensive battle response, so Lieutenant I am ordering that we drop the alert level and drop the shields."

The ships shields came down and the alert level dropped too 'yellow'[6].

While all this activity was happening throughout the ship, David was in the front section of the Astrophysics Lab with Dr. Schiller, the labs Lieutenant and chief scientist. They were both heavily involved in studying the active signals they had discovered, studying together for many hours and still unable to translate even one word.

Dr. Schiller had said to David that he thought the red alarm they heard was most likely a training exercise on the bridge and probably they weren't notified about the test due to their intense work. When the alarm rolled down to yellow David said he figured it would soon roll down to blue, plain old normal.

The lab seemed rather large right now to David, even with Dr. Schiller present. The viewport of the lab might as well have been a solid wall when they were working.

Suddenly, they were both thrown to the floor from a large bolting of the ship.

The alert went to Red, and the ships sirens matched the alert level in their loud, wavering shrill sound.

---

[6] "Yellow Alert Level" - Star Fleet Ship-wide state of increased preparedness for possible crisis situations.

Dr. Schiller got up from the floor and went over to his lab's consul, bringing up the ships active diagraming and couldn't believe what he was seeing. The diagram showed direct hits to the ships defensive computer system.

The weapons support pylons were flickering on the consul as they both were looking at it in utter shock and disbelief.

"My God," said Dr. Schiller, "the defense system is disintegrating[7]. David, I am giving you a direct order as a civilian which is to run like hell, right now, to Deck 6 and the aft hanger. You have been trained on the experimental life-pod, and I order you, David, to get in it and hit the red emergency button. Then, with the door sealed and yourself strapped in, and do that quickly, then if the pods computer decides you must abandon the ship, the pod will close if you have not closed it, followed by immediate ejection from the ship. I would tell you more but there is no more time. Run like hell David and stay out of the turbo-lifts. Go! Go David, GO!" yelled Dr. Schiller as loud as he could.

---

[7] The attacking ship may have been a Roman 'Scimitar' which could mimic a Star Fleet 'Miranda' class frigate.

CHAPTER 5

NEENSED

David woke up, blurry eyed for a few minutes, and feeling totally exhausted. As David became more aware of his surroundings he thought, not again, in another hospital. David thought this was all too familiar, yet this didn't look like the Baikonur hospital section. As David slowly looked around the room, he thought it looked more like a single bed intensive care unit. Then he noticed a young man apparently sitting at a desk station just on the other side of the glass wall who was then looking up from his work at David, immediately giving David a hand wave with joyful smile.

The man came into the room from his desk and introduced himself to David, "Wow, it is fantastic to see you're finally awake. My name is RhazLason[8] and I'm sure you want to know what's going on and where you're at. I am going to call NeenSed who has been waiting for you to wake up."

In a few minutes a tall and well-built blond-haired man came into the room, wearing a beautiful colored robe that reminded David of an African Dashiki. "Hello David, I am NeenSed. Correct me if I am wrong, but I believe your name is David Marcus? Right," asked NeenSed with his face expressing definite joy as he introduced himself to David.

---

[8] Rhazlason - Rhaz translates as Registered Nurse and Lason is the man's family name

"Yes sir, you're correct, my name is David Marcus, but David is just fine with me sir. It certainly doesn't look like I am on the Baikonur so where is this medical facility. How did I get here?"

NeenSed replied "I can help you with that David. First, let's begin with the fact that one of our scout ships picked-up a distress signal and the source of that signal was the life pod you were found in, a form of emergency survival craft. You were asleep, in a suspended state. Our ship, the "Tool-Lon", brought you here in that pod, in a suspended state. We studied your support system and figuring out how it functioned and soon we were able to remove you safely from it.

David, you have been in bed for three days now and finally here you are, awake and talking very well."

"Your name sir is pronounced 'neen said' asked David as his forehead wrinkled in a questioning attitude.

"Yes, that is partially right David. Let me explain a little. In our language spelling Neen begins with a capital N and then lower-case 'e e n' which translates into your English as 'mental health therapist'. I am like a psychologist or a psychiatrist in your culture. David, 'Sed' is spelled capital 'S' followed by lower case letters 'e' 'd'. So, David, Sed is my family name, like your last name of Marcus. We rarely use a first name in our culture." "This is almost too much for me. I can believe it but where is the rest of the Baikonur crew," asked David.

"Is our understanding, David, from our research, that your ship was totally destroyed and unfortunately it appears that you are the only survivor. I'm very sorry David," replied NeenSed.

David shook his head and said repeatedly, "no, no, no". David's eyes were glazed- over and his face was frozen from emotion.

NeenSed had to leave the unit and left the door open so RhazLason could hear anything from David.

The next morning, David was sitting up in his hospital bed and had just finished breakfast when NeenSed arrived at the door.

"David, I regret having to tell you the truth in answer to your question yesterday so abruptly, but I believe being direct was the only choice I had."

"Thank you NeedSed, thank you. But where am I? Sir, you appear to be human. And you speak English. So, I am surprised that we seem to be the same?" asked David.

"David, I began learning English in the past two years. My people recently discovered signals from your home planet, Earth. Oh, sorry David, that beep is to remind me that is it your scheduled physical therapy time. I might be around after lunch, okay David?" asked NeenSed. "Yes, thank you," replied David.

The next few days NeenSed and David meet for some light conversations on whatever subject David brought up, including much of his past, even about Marian.

After a couple of intense weeks in physical therapy and casual conversation with NeenSed, David decided it was time to learn what was going to happen to him.

At David's request he got to enjoy a relaxing lunch with NeenSed away from the medical unit. Lunch was on a furnished floor that was like a beautiful lounge. David was looking out the glass wall on what appeared to be a rain forest. They were both sitting and enjoying what David thought was the most delicious coffee he could remember ever having. This tasted like his old favorite, Italian Roast, but so much better. While enjoying this escape David was just awestruck at the view.

"Well, NeenSed, I can honestly say that I have never seen such a beautiful landscape and that beautiful city off in the distance. The light glimmering on those gorgeous structures to me looks like diamond stones in a ring. But I do have a question, NeenSed, about an experience I'm having here that is odd to me." "And what is that David," replied NeenSed.

David replied, "no matter where I have been in this hospital, whether walking around or in physical therapy or for that matter even in my unit, have I ever seen a woman. I never heard anyone talk about a wife, daughter, or girlfriend. I asked a couple of my nurses about their dating or wives, and I was told they are not allowed to talk about their private lives. So, am I in some form of social isolation?"

"No David, you're not in isolation. But you are in an isolation for your own safety and ours due to all the medical un-knowns'. None of us have been physically near one of your species and vice-versa for that. So medical safety is a priority as our scientists study your blood and all we can learn from that. There simply are unknowns David. As for myself, when I leave this area, I go through a sterilization procedure and must wait for a short time after that for safety clearance. So far, I have had no contamination issues of any type, or I would be residing here in this unit".

"I would guess that all those dealing with me go through that sterilization process," asked David.

"You're right David, absolutely correct. And now if you're okay with it, I will begin slowly but surely getting deep into our history with you and eventually answering some of your' questions. This will take some time, more than a few days is my guess."

"NeenSed I'm ready to hear it all. This will beat looking at the four walls." replied David with a slight giggle and then asking for another cup of coffee.

CHAPTER 6

BathKohl
"An Interplanetary Society"

"David, you are on my home planet, BathKohl, which is now part of an interplanetary society. We have been interplanetary in trading for a few centuries now. I would say that less than 80 years ago BathKohl got the incentive to form more legally set relationships with other planets which lead to the formation of "The Interplanetary Society".

Why this all came about was that over time we met other space exploring ships from various planets which gave us all the opportunity to develop very positive trade relations. With those trade relations it became apparent that we had a need to form a unifying governing body. It took a couple of years and soon we all formed "The Interplanetary Society", as we named it.

All the planets involved had forms of elected governing bodies which truly made it much easier in forming this union. A process for periodically electing a Governing Council with a body President was formed and universally adopted by all.

Unfortunately, many years after this wonderful success my home-world of BathKohl and our colonized planets would be expelled from that "Society" which were our major trading partners. David, do you want me to continue or are you ready for a break?"

"I would love to hear more if you don't mind NeenSed."

"Okay David, on we go. About the time this great union was nearing its completion, BathKohl discovered 3 planets that were a definite scientific surprise to us all. This was a huge unexpected find as the three of them were found to be excellent subjects for terraforming. The research concluded that none of the three had any life forming foundation. In time we colonized two of the three and had a very good and healthy migration from BathKohl. We decided to wait on the third terraforming planet to extend our study of its development without any colonization. "

"Are you serious Neensed, you're already into terraforming? I want to hear much more about that," broke in David, definitely surprised.

"David, your excitement is amazing. If you have patience enough, I will slowly get into our history, okay David?"

"Yes, I can wait, barely. I will find patience somehow," replied David.

Then on we go David, "In our continuing planetary exploration, we found histories of active waring federations and planets. I believe your federation may also have made such discoveries, would that be right David?"

"Yes, that's right NeenSed, I have been thinking that maybe it is time for you to ask me some questions which I'll answer as best I can," replied David.

"I do have a few curiosities, David. I am wondering what is "Astrophysics within your Star Fleet," NeenSed asked while getting up out of his chair for a little coffee and some light snacks from the serving cart. David's reply was for more cold water which NeenSed brought over and handed to David, and then returned to his chair.

"Thanks for the water, NeenSed. I do have two love affairs which are astrophysics and terraforming. I think it is safe to say that in Star Fleet

Astrophysics has its beginning in astronomy on Earth. The development of physics on my home planet of Earth led to our studying of all types of objects being discovered in our older history and in our more modern travels throughout our solar system and eventually into other parts of our galaxy, which we call the Milky Way. NeenSed, our Federation officially formed in 2161 of our Earth calendars. The Federation was formed in San Francisco, California. But our Federation, unlike the peaceful origin of your federation, developed out of the Earth-Romulan War.

The formation of our Federation was, as I see it, the solid beginning of Astrophysics. I have been attracted to astrophysics from the early years of my youth and I have been its student all my life. I had a full scholarship, which means all my costs were paid to attend "the Daystrom Institute" on our planet Mars. I was blessed beyond my dreams to be able to transfer my studies to the USS Baikonur which went on a deep space mission, and I was aiming at acquiring a doctoral degree in astrophysics while on the Baikonur. On the Baikonur I had regularly scheduled tests and reports to complete which were communicated back to my instructors at the Daystrom Institute on Mars.

NeenSed, while on the Baikonur I was unexpectedly assigned to study and be part of the Stellar Cartography research. At first, I wasn't so sure about adding more studies but as I moved along in Stellar Cartography, I realized how important it was to my studies in astrophysics."

"NeenSed, I must tell you before we go any further that our talking is definitely helping me be far more comfortable and getting me past my drama and I really appreciate that, thank you," said David.

"Thank you, David. Helping you find a path out of your personal pain is truly my purpose here. I also would like to say that I believe we have developed a great friendship," said NeenSed.

"I agree NeenSed," responded David.

"David, I will carry on with a more of this history and begin with what I know about your arrival to our planetary system. You are the first from your planet that has been in our galactic location let alone here on my home world, BathKohl. If your ship had continued its projected path, you would have entered into our home system," said NeenSed.

David replied in a very serious tone, "then what would bring a ship of yours to attack our ship?"

To that question NeenSed replied, "No David, we would have never attacked your ship excluding an undeniable need for a defensive action. Due to our well- developed defensive array your Baikonur would never have received any images of our home planetary system. That array would have projected a signal for you to follow that which have taken your vessel away from our system. Our defense system would have placed emptiness on all visual systems of your ship, no visible planet bodies, no Sun, no stars, just empty space "

"Wow, that is amazing NeenSed, an empty screen. Perhaps Sir, you can arrange for me to see that defensive system?" asked David.

"No to that David. That I can say for sure is against our security regulations. As is said here 'when unnecessary it should not be,' replied NeenSed, "and I have no doubt David that you will receive no exception to these rules."

"I can live with that NeenSed. So, how about we get back into your history."

"Sure David. I have observed that there are many similarities between our societies. Our biology is like yours. But I think for now I will head back into that arena of astrophysics. I think it is okay to share with you David that we have had great success in our terraforming. My grandfather was considered the leader in our planetary terraforming."

David broke in and said, "I must tell you NeenSed that what you're doing in terraforming is exactly what my mother has been trying to develop for many years."

"I know I brought up terraforming earlier but nonetheless, I would have never guessed that your people are working on terraforming. David, you said your mother is managing terraforming. What is her name David?" asked NeenSed.

"My mother's name is Dr. Carol Marcus, and she has what we call a Doctoral Degree in Astrophysics and one in Bio Forming. My mother also has an important expertise in Molecular Biology. She told me before I set off on the Baikonur that she was very challenged in discovering the foundation for her terraforming goal, but she knew she would get there. And NeenSed, my mother is part of our Star Fleet 'Terraform Command' which is the administrative governing body over our terraforming," replied David.

NeenSed replied, "I would have never dreamed of this David.

I think your mother is amazing. Was this ship, your Baikonur, involved with your Star Fleet terraforming research?"

"No Sir, we were exploring what we call the Alpha Quadrant of our Milky Way Galaxy, exploring the truly unknown, totally exciting," answered David.

"I'm beginning to feel like I am on your Baikonur mission. It's definitely time for a break. I need a snack and some fresh water, but I think I have had more than enough coffee for now. And then when your' ready, we can decide who gets to ask the first question. David, let's take a short break."

"Great, I need a break," said David as he got up from his comfortable chair and strolled down the hall heading for as he called it, a nature break. He had no trouble finding the Men's Room as he looked around the immediate area for a women's restroom sign and could find none.

He returned to the lounge, grabbed a bottle of water and sat down slowly into his chair.

C H A P T E R 7

"FEAR AND REPRESSION"

"I wonder NeenSed, if you now could answer my earlier question as to why I have not seen any women in this wing of your hospital and neither the slightest conversation about a woman," asked David.

"Good question David but that answer will take some time which I will eventually get too. So, first I will order lunch and there are snacks on the cart right now David.

Coffee is ready and bottled water is in the cooler drawer." "Well, patience is my middle name right now NeenSed. Tell you what, I'll take one of those great tasty snacks and pour myself some coffee and grab a bottle of water. Please go ahead and carry on NeenSed."

"Where to start David, let's see. Our history was very normal, peaceful, and productive, before and after we became an interplanetary society. From what we learned in a few centuries of interplanetary travel and the unexpected successes of our planets and our trading partners, including our federation, led us into an extraordinary rewarding life with a continuing peaceful history. In our interplanetary adventures of the unknown we have never been involved in any type of conflict with other planets or other groups that we have met.

But, sadly David, our many, many years of peace, somehow, we became our own worst enemy here on BathKohl. It's a very shattering history of ourselves. Looking back on that history I can say in that my humble opinion that some people are imprisoned by what they believe to be freedom.

BathKohl and our other inhabited planets had various religious and spiritual paths. No one on BathKohl had ever heard of interfering with another person's belief or spiritual path. Such events had never been part of our history.

And now David I need to pour myself another coffee and get another bottled water and a sandwich. And if it is alright with you, I'm going to pass my history hat over to you for some more of your history, all right David?"

"Okay NeenSed, your student will take your hat for a while.

I believe it is fair to say that of my home planet, Earth, I see we have a similar history. On Earth we had a historical problem we call proselytizing which truly interfered with individual rights. In our history we have a long line of persecution in different cultures and beliefs. In my history studies there was this evangelizing by many young men and women which brought me down to a level of quiet fear and mistrust. NeenSed, where would you like me to go next in this exchange," asked David as he sat gently back in his chair, taking notice of NeenSed with that beautiful city view behind him.

"David, I've been thinking about a few things and if it's not too much, I am wondering about your ships name, your Star Fleet Academy, and your organization of the United Federation of Planets. I am curious about what similarities there are between our societies," replied NeenSed.

"The ship I was on was named 'the USS Baikonur' which was an exploration craft of the United Federation of Planets. USS means 'United Star Ship' and the U refers to the 'United Federation of Planets'. So technically NeenSed, one would correctly call the Baikonur, "the United

Star Ship Baikonur". "Baikonur" is truly a name from the very beginning of our space program of Earth. Baikonur was the "Baikonur Cosmodrome of the former Soviet Union, which is presently called "Russia".

The "Baikonur Cosmo Drome" was the launch complex where the first Earth space program began with the launch of Earth's first artificial satellite, Sputnik 1. The first human to go into orbit around our Earth was also launched from the Baikonur, his name being Yuri Gagarin. Baikonur was the location of all Russian crewed missions and many other types of launches, and those which lead to our first International Space Station, and I must include lunar and planetary explorations, usually unmanned. This center included launching for the United States and many other nations.

Eventually, of all places, Bozeman, Montana will be the center of change in our space program with the break-thru of light speed space travel. Faster than light space travel was endlessly talked about in our government and public, written about, and lost in one government committee after another.

Bozeman, Montana, was the home to the study of Solar Physics and part of that research program was funded in the early 20th century by NASA which was then the space program of the United States.

In 2053 Zefram Cochrane recruited a scientific engineering support group outside Bozeman, Mt., and in their isolation and secrecy, they acquired an unlisted and hidden missile silo that contained a Titan II nuclear missile which became the "Phoenix". Cochrane and his staff created the first flight out of a missile silo bringing Earth its first ever successful 'faster-than-light' warp-drive on April fifth of 2063, thus culminating 10 years of unceasing and undisclosed work which was hidden from everyone outside Cochrane's staff. The only ones who knew were those who made it happen.

More of that later but I will get on with the United Federation of Planets. That first warp drive success, piloted by Zefram Cochrane himself, was observed by a Vulcan ship, bringing the earth into its first interplanetary experience. Cochrane was the first of our planet Earth to meet an extraterrestrial. The Vulcan Solkar and Zefram celebrated their meeting by going to a bar and both drinking many beers.

Out of the meeting of Cochrane and Sokar came our Federation which is very similar to your Planetary Union, and our Federation was more like our United Nations structure with a little of the European Union. In a sense, our Federation became a United Nations of our Milky Way Galaxy.

Star Fleet than is the Federations outer space exploratory division and the Federations military defense system, we have exploration and military defense combined into one functioning group."

NeenSed interrupted David asking, "David, was the Baikonur a military vessel?"

David answered NeenSed's question, stating, "that the Baikonur was an explorative vessel and only had a defensive weapons system."

NeenSed interrupted David and asked, "David, my curiosity is on what happened that you were ejected in that Life-Pod?"

"I was on duty in the ships Astrophysics Lab when the ship rocked violently, and Dr. Schiller ordered me to immediately go to the Life-Pod which I did. I followed Dr. Schiller's order and got into the Life-Pod and no sooner then I entered the Life-Pod that it suddenly closed and the engines fired-up. Apparently, the Life-Pod's computer decided to put me into stasis immediately. The next memory I have is waking up here in your medical unit," answered David.

"Thank you, David, for being so honest. Do you have any idea who attacked your ship with such unfortunate destruction?" asked NeenSed.

"It's a total mystery to me to this very day. And I am still a little shook-up about being the only survivor as I feel guilty about being the only survivor. Depression definitely hits me hard then, but I look at the present to break those shackles."

"David, that is another reason that I am always available for you, at all times," NeenSed stated quietly while embracing David's right hand.

"Thank you NeenSed. I think our sharing like we have been doing is a tremendous and unexpected help to me,' replied David while looking at their clasped hands with a gentle smile as he felt very welcomed and safe like he never had since waking up in the unit. "Would you like to take a break David," asked NeenSed.

"I think I would like to continue NeenSed. I doubt I would get any sleep at all with my questions waiting in the wing," replied David.

"I will continue in a few minutes, but I was thinking, how would you like a cold glass of wine, David?" asked NeenSed.

"Oh, wow, that would be great. Thank you. I can't remember the last time I enjoyed a glass of wine," said David.

"Let's have a light snack along with wine. Give me a minute and I will make the call for a good drink," said NeenSed.

A marvelously handsome server entered the lounge and placed a beautiful crystal filled wine glass at each side table along with a few snacks. NeenSed was looking at the server as he exited and said, "thank you so much." "You're both welcomed" said the server as he exited the door.

David was looking with great appreciation at NeenSed, saying, "Cheers and salute my good friend."

"Thank you, David, thank you," replied NeenSed as they both raised their wine glasses to each other. David rarely drank any alcohol beverages and declined a refill, stating that one had given him a little buzz and that was great but quite enough.

"Okay David, my turn to play history teacher so I'll take my hat back. I can say that I will never understand how this home of mine, BathKohl, would ever see a violent revolution, but two generations back after thousands of years of peace, our history became a real living hell for all of us, in opinion anyway.

My family's hometown is called "Atum"[9], spelled in your English, capital 'A' and then lower case 't u m'. That word is the same as your word 'atom' as in your Nuclear Physics. Unlike your history with the atomic bomb, our scientists were looking for an energy source for space travel.

About 360 years ago in your time our government began to turn to a totally unknown and never-before experienced conservative attitude, leaning towards a one-party control of both politics and religion, unifying them into one controlling body. This rising conservative government wanted to further terraform on other planets if possible, and then beyond my understanding, end our interplanetary trading system. Eventually, due to this odd conservative movement our integrated planets would be expelled from the Federation we were so central to in its formation." "NeenSed, you're bringing me to wonder what your life span is here on BathKohl," asked David.

"We average a good 180 year's, David," answered NeenSed.

"180 years, I want that for damned sure NeenSed. Our best is 100 years, maybe 120 if you're truly lucky. But if you can double that for me, NeenSed, I will take it," David replied with a light laugh and large smile.

"David, I think adding years is a little out of our ability right now. As for my personal great science, I'm pretty much just an old-fashioned mental health therapist." NeenSed was relaxing more in his chair, placing his hands behind his head and feet up on the pop-out footrest. "And on we go David, into more history. We had various religious and spiritual paths in our civilization and never in our known history had there been any conflict of anyone's private or group belief or having no religious nor spiritual belief for that matter. I can say that one was equally respected if you just lay under a tree or travel to the stars. Throughout our system equality was and is again about possibilities and potential, and the celebration of difference, and difference being the greatest teacher. When I was a preschooler, I remember my grandfather saying to me 'that freedom is the gift to live life unafraid and untethered'. I never

---

[9] "Atum" - translates as 'Atom', NeenSed's home town.

forgot what he said but some years passed before I truly understood what he meant.

Now, this new rising conservative movement eventually took control of our BathKohl's governing system and claiming our terraformed planets along with our two colonized planets.

David, most of us were so busy with our research that most of us never really understood the changes that were blatantly obvious."

David broke in saying, "NeenSed you stated that your terraformed planets also were taken under control of this rising power. Are you saying two of your terraformed planets had actually been colonized?"

"Yes David, we had colonized two planets that were extremely successful in terraforming. My grandfather was the team leader and simply the best researcher in his work. Both planets owed their terraforming success to him and his research staff."

"I know you have mentioned this terraforming before but to understand your grandfather's success is important to me. I would like to know more about that since it is my life's love affair, my work" replied David.

"David, I will have to go through our security and find out what our science may be allowed to share with you on that. My guess is right now that it will be at least a week before I get an answer on this, but I will submit your request this evening."

"That is great NeenSed, thanks!" replied David, who was absolutely thrilled.

"Alright David, putting my professor's hat back on I will take back my turn in teaching. In reflection, I can say that some people are imprisoned by what they believe to be freedom without ever realizing it. I think that those who were rising to power here on BathKohl knew without any doubt that their most powerful weapon was reverence. When those individuals rose to the illusion of power, they were separate from the simplicity of honesty and its empowering core of truth. Citizens were slowly becoming infected with this devotion to a theocratic governing body. Their movement became known as "RenCeti[10]".

David, RenCeti was, as I look back, the perfect title, as it means 'water frozen'. That was the appropriate title as our lives were becoming frozen. It took some time before we recognized we were becoming stiff and frozen."

David's response was, "that really scares me as it reminds me partly of our own Earth history. But I am really locked into this history of yours. Please carry on my good friend."

"David, as that rising conservative system grew in power so did the judgement and intolerance of any religious or spiritual belief outside of this new religion of "RenCeti". This RenCeti body began to write into our legal code their prejudices of belief and judgement which was becoming their structured theology and dogma.

Eventually 'RenCeti' decided they're developing theology and dogma was the only valid belief that any citizen of BathKohl and its colonized planets, terraformed or not, could practice, publicly or privately.

Most of our citizens did not take any of this seriously. I remember my parents telling me at our dinner table one evening that this supposed legal action was the strangest action of any type in our history. My Dad thought this would be overturned soon, either politically or through the legal system, or just wear itself out.

My dad's name was NeenBonSed which translates as 'Neen', as you have been told is therapist, and BonSed translates as 'father of the Sed family'. My mother's name was MarinZhifronSed which translates as translates as "wife from the family Zhifron, wife of Sed".

---

[10] RenCeti - translates as "Water Frozen". Ran was the title of the religious organization and Ceit refers to the governing body, the rising dogmatic governing body of planet BathKohl.

In a short period of time, it became apparent to all that this 'RenCeti' movement now successfully controlled our governing body and the legal system. I think because few of us took this seriously that when the power structure completely adapted too 'RenCeti' it was a shock to everyone. Soon fear and repression would become our social norm.

My parents decided to take the pledge to this new government, therefore, essentially to RenCeti. They told me later that they did this to protect me. I can see an odd look on your face David. So, what are you thinking?" asked NeenSed.

"I was wondering how your family made it through that horrible time," David asked of Sed.

"Thank you, David. I learned from my parents that taking any pledge or signing any document as required, kept them safe. In extreme quiet, my parents were looking for a group that they could join in resistance to this RenCeti, but they could not find any group they could trust. My father said that the very least they did was pray for a return to the society that was now lost. Protecting me was their first choice and for that I am very grateful.

I remember a conversation one night at our dinner table when I had just entered what is equal to your Junior High. Dad was talking about the difficulty of appearing to be a true follower in the RenCeti and yet looking for some way to act against this system. I asked him once how he continued living in this regret and his answer amazed me. I never want to forget what he said which was, "it is not living correctly that is justified, but rather living rightly." Regardless of my parent's outward appearance my dad lived in strong anger while waiting for some type of massive revolution.

Mother told me that their parent's spiritual family they had been born into from was named ShaneTahn which means "Life's Center". They were a metaphysical group which had their own rituals that could be changed as the members found a need to change.

It is hard to believe that things could get worse, but they did. It wasn't too long when planets in our trading system and our Foundation broke off all trading and diplomatic relations with BathKohl. That happened shortly after our two terraformed planets joined the RenCeti. Our Federation was totally staggered by this change taking place on BathKohl and our mutual planets.

The trading losses were devastating to our economy. There were so many items which we acquired only through trade which we had no way of replacing.

In RenCeti's third year of control the RenCeti made it absolute law that anyone who had converted into that required belief would be in grave sin if they left RenCeti. Even worse consequences if they returned to their previous beliefs again or had the courage to believe they could create a new spiritual path.

As I understand our history, underneath the governing body of RenCeti, an anger to re-gain the freedom of our past was growing, isolated in growing strength.

To RenCeti, "Fear is Freedom which becomes its greatest Strength". What better control could one devise.

Soon all spiritual and religious centers were ordered to be permanently closed but could remain open if they became Centers of RenCeti.

Spiritual leaders and ministers who did not convert to RenCeti were placed under house-arrest. Their staffs were arrested and soon imprisoned if they did not quickly convert.

Soon it became the norm that anyone found in public not carrying a RenCeti membership card was immediately placed under house arrest and if you did not follow the rules of house-arrest you also would be picked-up and placed in prison.

This repressive nightmare continued to grow. In the beginning of the fourth year under RenCeti, anyone caught participating in civil disobedience, protest, or any type of civil demonstration against RenCeti was automatically guilty of grave sin and was executed on the spot, whether that was a single person or a group. There was no concern about age or sex. This was a success by RenCeti as our defense system became a military arm of the RenCeti theology and governing body. RenCeti quickly spread throughout our planetary system.

Civil war was smoldering quietly in the hot coals of fear that were stoked throughout our system. That war slowly began here on BathKohl and with little effort it spread through fertilized strength and courage. Strength and courage from something no one had thought of before, love for our history and our mutual respect in all affirming life choices.

GRANDFATHER SED AND REVOLUTION

"Hello David, I see you're ready for lunch following yesterday and my lengthily history class."

"Hi NeenSed. Again, I didn't know how long we went yesterday until I sat down for dinner and was so tired, I didn't want to take a shower, but I did. I will set up my lunch and I'm ready to hear more. This is so amazing, and I truly appreciate your sharing your history with me. Thank you again NeenSed."

"No problem, David. How is the burger?"

"Just great, my favorite lunch. And with those milk shakes, mmm mm," said David as he sipped his filled espresso cup. you're spoiling me NeenSed, and I love it. Carry on NeenSed, please."

"David, I will open today's history lesson with action by my grandfather, RonSed. Ron means grandfather in our language but in formality his name is very long. I will explain that. His formal name is AhbenRaRonSed.

To begin with, the word terraforming in our language is 'AhbendPres' which I believe you pronounce as 'ah bend freeze'.

NeenSed, looking at David said, "as I understand from what you've said David, your mother has two degrees, one being in terraforming the other in bio forming. Our degree in terraforming would be like combining your mothers two degrees into one. Am I right on that David?"

"Yes, your right on that NeenSed," replied David.

"My grandfather's degree title is placed in front of his family name, Ron. His degree title in our terraforming is 'AhbendRa'. His full name is AhbendRaRonSed[11].

In this growing nightmare here on BathKohl those placed under house arrest were given set times for shopping to acquire food or any other needs. Medical care was refused to all under house arrest regardless of any personal consequences, unless they converted. Those who were given the responsibility to decide if the conversion was honest and true would be the final word as to freedom within RenCeti or if they must remain under house arrest.

For those under house-arrest that claimed conversion but were believed to be dishonest were immediately executed by order of the controlling body of RenCeti.

This nightmare of oppression continued to grow and as my parents said to me, "they found what was happening to be staggering and absolutely unbelievable".

One day it was ruled from RenCeti that of the "converted", anyone having no desire to create children or apparently not doing so in their marriage were placed into assignments such as military and policing duty.

My grandfather lived on our second transformed planet which was named "RaedenOvul". When at home during any conversation about my grandfather on RaedenOvul, I always called RaedenOvul "my grandfather's planet". I would only say that when I was alone with

____

[11] AhbendRaRonSed - NeenSed's Grandfather's full name (Doctor of Terraforming Grandfather Sed)

my parents because if others heard me saying that my family probably would have been held in house-arrest.

"RaedenOvul" translates in your English as "created Seed".

Apparently, my grandfather and his staff on "RaedenOvul" were of such great importance to RenCeti that they were left alone, never threatened or harassed. I think that RenCeti figured their terraforming work would expand the power of RenCeti.

There is no doubt that without RonSed's work there would have been no terraforming in our planet's history.

History revealed a new view as courage grew amongst a few on BathKohl and on "RaedenOvul", RonSed's home where he lived on with his terraforming crew.

RonSed told me onetime when there was talk about revolution "that making a good decision and then taking the necessary action from that decision can seem extremely negative and upsetting. Regardless of how right the decision is the proper choice can become a struggle with low self-esteem. He said fear wasn't the enemy but making a bad decision out of fear just wasn't right. But when you act on the right decision you garner strength out of your fear regardless of the result of the right choice.

My grandfather told me that that he had considered becoming part of the revolution despite what it would cost him, if even his life. I kept this a secret as what I had been told would cost my families safety and probably their lives.

How time and history changes. I have spoken lightly of revolution so far but shortly after talking to RonSed, revolution began to show itself on BathKohl.

Our capital on BathKohl is NorisColre[12] which translates as

---

[12] NorisColren - "Talking Center", the Capitol of planet BathKohl.

"Talking center". Oh David, that was such a beautiful city. From a distance it had the reflection you have enjoyed out this window so often."

David interrupted NeenSed asking, "NeenSed, what is the name of the city where you were at?"

"It is our rebuilt Capitol city, NorisColren, and what you're seeing outside is the central district of NorisColren. This medical facility where we are at right now is on the edge of the city." "NeenSed, you said rebuilt. What happened?" asked David.

"Shortly after my last communication with my RonSed, the revolution actually started in the central core of NorisColren with a large attack on the central building which would be like your national capitol building in your U.S. I remember the live news cast at my parent's home, and it was like this;

"Children of Ren, Ladies and gentlemen, we are called here today in RenTahn to live our responsibility in governing, we the blessed in the light of Ren, the water of our souls.

Let us hold hands as we unite together within Ren. And now we must hold council as we extend the word on BathKohl and our other planetary bodies. And then we shall move as we are gifted too," stated QuanRen their High Priestess. "What is the word on our needs of this day QuanRen[13]?" asked the many in the hall.

QuaRen, looking at SironLashval[14], "I would like to know from our 'Guardians of the Word and the life of RenCeti', how is our present security in regards' to any problems. Blessed we are the many converted in their desert of loss here on BathKohl. And second, how are we doing on RaedenOvul as the word, our True Water of Ren blesses so many.'"

---

[13] "QuaRen" - Translates as "Voice of the Water" (Ren) - position title "Founders Prophet" and High Priestess of Ren.

[14] "SironLashval '"Siron" is the 'leading voice of the Guardians (like a police force Captain). 'Lashval' meaning 'valley'.

SironLashval rose to answer QuaRen, "my dear QuaRen, our acceptance of AhbendRaRonSed and his staff in their unbelievable success in AhbendPres can only help us expand the 'Water'.

To date, this is the only group that is capable of our successful terraforming. No one has yet acquired the knowledge of AhbendRaRonSed. He is the central core to our terraforming. We have added new members to his staff and regardless of their studies and degrees, so far no one else has been gifted to have his knowledge.

"SironLashval, what of our terraforming team on RaedenOvul, have they converted?" asked QuaRen.

"To our knowledge QuaRen, as of last month no members of that team have converted, to our Gift in this Water, to our freedom," replied SironLashval.

"SironLashval, and my friends listening in this hall, our "Water" as we have been taught to express will make more converts than I would think. It may be that those on RaedenOvul are so central to creation that the "Word of Water" will be expressed from them as they create. Only in our temple and with myself present will there ever be any discussion of those in creation on RaedenOvul," said QuaRen.

"And so, it shall be" replied all in the hall.

"SironLashval, how does the conversion of Water flow on our BathKohl today?" asked QuaRen.

"QuaRen, I find my spirit hurts in the truth of many that refuse "our Water". We work with those that stay in shoals or hide upon the shores. We have continued to work with isolating those who will not convert in hope that they will one day find conversion to be celebrated here at our Temple, our wellspring.

SironLashval looked more to the others in attendance over the right shoulder of QuaRen than looking QuaRen in her eyes, "My Priestess, I believed that in a short time many in doubt would convert but this has not proven true. As we know, previously there were many on numerously different false belief paths and many who choose no path."

Suddenly, under the Temple RenTahn's amphitheater seating, numerous large explosions erupted and lifted the structures support beams up and through the temple itself.

The amphitheater was nearly full as the temple lifted-up high off its foundation structure and disintegrated.

The explosion was heard throughout capitol city and as far away as NeenSed's hometown of Atum. NeenSed's parents dropped what they were doing and immediately got on their public transportation and went to their capital of NorisColren. Many went to the Temple RenTahn to help in the rescue.

The RenCeti Temple had formerly been BathKohl's Capitol building. The structure was a huge smoky, flaming pile of debris from under which moans and cries for help could heard, blood was splattered throughout the debris.

This had never happened in any of our history, David, and remembering what I have heard, it was a carnage beyond imagination. A strong disgusting stench settled in surrounding the Temple.

Screams of painful dread echoed off the debris while consternation spread through the air from those approaching the disaster, a catastrophe not understood by anyone.

The setting sun was red as the smoke formed the appearance of thunderheads while all local lighting systems were out in the surrounding area as well as all communications systems.

Rescuers found it very difficult to approach the disaster because of the horrific damage within a two-block radius of the temple. The area had been filled with beams, fractured walls, furniture, and occasional bodies; survivors were a rare find in the rubble.

As rescuers climbed over the debris to get to the Temple some were injured as portions of the rubble unexpectedly shifted. As many of the rescuers broke through the surrounding debris, the nightmare of the temple left many speechless as their capitol building of NorisColren had been destroyed.

A few rescuers borrowed a couple of neighboring vehicles and made it to the nearby Interspace Construction Center. They managed to get five construction ships who flew in overheard and hovered in place above the Temple.

The construction vehicles were able to remove various debris, lifting the debris carefully over to their Interspace Construction Center.

The Sun rose in a red-blooded texture within the appearance of thick thunder- clouds being formed from the heavy smoke. A plan had been devised to remove the wreckage with help from the neighborhood while medical aid was on site for survivors. The dead far outnumbered the survivors and were quickly bagged and moved to the outer perimeter.

In the late afternoon of the second day numerous large pieces of rubble had been successfully removed and everyone on site was stunned as the "Founders Prophet", QuaRen, was found alive and conscious in the rubble. A dismayed silence struck all the rescuers. The QuaRen was immediately flown to the nearest medical center while many of the rescuers fell into unified prayer for the QuaRen.

Chapter 9

The Aberration of Wisdom

Following the rescue and burials a month later, the temple site had been filled with soil while the rubble had been left in place. A temporary seating form of an open stadium style was placed on the site while many flags of the RenCeti symbol were placed throughout the seating.

"It is your resolve that has led us to this moment, a manifestation of our mutual reverent devotion. This truly is our first experience that we are all one family, we are "RenCeti"! And I, you're QuaRen, give thanks to you all.

It took a vile deed upon which memory we now stand to bind us together into a flotilla upon the waters of our lives. And now, let us hold hands in silent reverence of our losses. They held hands and were swaying left and right in an apparent unity of love.

For some of those holding hands their quiet love was not for the high priestess nor this religion but in suffering memory of their lost culture, their lost life.

A few minutes into the silence there were some faces of concern and confusion as they could hear screams in the surrounding distance.

QuaRen raised her hands and said to those in attendance, "I, your QuaRen, the voice of 'the Water' must say that "Our Water" is called 'Frozen Water" for it is the one and only path of our spirit. I now state that for those who by my word, dwell in sin and refuse to join us in the flow of 'the Water will in their souls be set free, the souls of their families, and the souls of their children. They will know the strength and depth of our Water."

Further into this quiet moment many holding hand in hand in silence expressed concern and confusion on their faces as they heard screams in the immediate neighborhood.

"I thank you for your labor, all of you, for your hours of care in this unacceptable and totally evil devastation of our temple, RenTahn. Our Sanctity will not be desecrated. I am "the voice of the water" and the flowing of our stream will not be defiled or obstructed in any way," said QuaRen as she lowered her hands which was the signal that all could now leave, in silence.

Heading home, NeenBonSed ran into a member of the Guardian who was long-time close friend and asked his Guardian friend what he might know about the load noises that sounded like hand-held weapons fire.

Their Guardian friend told him that by command of "The QuaRen", many in their hometown of Atom had been put to death that had refused for some time to join RenCeti.

He stated that those executed had been asked how they felt about the temple's destruction and those with no reply of remorse were immediately put to death. The bodies were to be left lying uncovered in front of their homes to express the anger of "the QuaRen", and according to her, their sins.

She said that any act of betrayal as she judged it would be met by immediately freeing the soul of the betrayer.

The Sed's quietly went home and after entering their residence, they held each other in sobbing tears. They had no regrets for the rescue work they had done but that good work had now come to a closure, an anguish of loss and increasing fear.

The following morning the Sed's Guardian friend dropped by for coffee and conversation.

"Neen, thank you for this great coffee. If you'll give me a moment. I just turned on my listening silencer before we continue our conversation. I'm not sure if there is a recording broadcast device in your house but I wouldn't be surprised. I know that many homes of RenCeti members have recording broadcast devices hidden in them. They were placed in numerous homes while you and others were aiding in the rescue. I'm so sorry but the QuaRen ordered the Guardian to do so. If one didn't do as she ordered, execution was her immediate response.

I suspect a Guardian member placed a listening device in your house and what I just turned on blocks the system with a hissing sound as if it has a malfunction. Not bad!"

"Well, I guess I can call you Shawn right now and ask what this secrecy is all about," asked NeenBonSed of his Guardian friend, Shawn.

"Neen," replied Shawn, "I have heard on the rumor line that this unexpected ongoing violence is energizing an outright revolutionary movement. Neen, have you smelled anything odd outside in your neighborhood since yesterday?"

"Yes, I have. Especially after my Marin said there was a stench in the backyard, and she could find nothing dead in the yard. She has been so disgusted with the smell that she closed all our windows and asked me to leave them closed. I went outback and there is a disgusting stench everywhere," replied Neen.

"Where's Marin Neen?" asked Shawn.

"She's upstairs and will be down in a minute. I better fix her coffee right now," replied Neen.

As Sed prepared Marin's coffee, she entered the kitchen, saying, "Ah, Neen, thank you, I need a good cup of hot coffee, especially with my body chill. "Hi Shawn, I thought I heard you come in. I know what that is, a blocking device for listening. Why Shawn?"

"I believe listening devices have been concealed here in your house and if you'll give me a few minutes, I will use this item to scan and see if my suspicion is correct. So, give me a minute," said Shawn as he quietly moved around the house looking for video and audio recording devices.

"Neen, I have found two well-hidden audio recorders and no video recorders. The must have been put into place while you were in the rescue work. This was well done, I must say. I am grateful your both still alive, and I know you haven't said anything that is seen as threatening," said Shawn as he looked at Neen and his wife.

"All right you two, I am going to turn off this disruptor in a minute and I am here to just thank you for your work in our rescue, ok?" said Shawn. "Got ya," replied Neen.

After Shawn got the disruptor turned off Need said, "Welcome to our home, Guardian. And how may we help you and our QuaRen?"

"I was in the neighborhood and wanted to drop in to thank you both for your work in the rescue after our temple was destroyed. So, thank you both very much. And I believe I can say thank you also for the QuaRen," said Guardian Shawn to the Seds.

"Guardian Shawn, I can definitely say that we are both grateful for your words and blessed to have flowed in the water to be part of the rescue. The temple may have been destroyed but our hearts have no disturbance in the flow as our trust is in the QuaRen," said Neen.

"Your most welcome family Sed. The answer to your question on the bodies in the neighborhood is that they will be removed tomorrow around sunrise. Be at peace and with the flow of the QuaRen. Goodbye," and Guardian Shawn left by the front door, when he opened it the air that came was unwelcome as it carried the stench of decaying bodies.

The next morning Sed and Marin were holding hands, having breakfast, and locked in silence as they listened to the vehicles driving through the neighborhood, stopping all too often as they picked up those that had been executed throughout the neighborhood.

Marin looked deeply into Sed's eyes, placed her coffee cup gently down on the table and got up for a short moment, walked over to the music center and turning a quiet mood music on and up very loud, returned to the table and kissing Sed gently, asking, "what do we do now my love, our society can't go on like this, we can't! How do we communicate with anyone? We don't have a community anymore. Some-how Sed, we have to wake-up from this nightmare, we have to!"

"Marin, would you lighten up on my hand, you've really been squeezing my hand. Whew, thanks Marin. I don't know what to say. I want our path back, I want ShaneTahn, and I prefer it yesterday, Marin, yesterday. If anyone is doing anything, outside those bombers, I believe it would be RaRon. RenCeti, truthfully I believe many more of us will be killed until what we had before this QuaRen and her RenCeti, is resurrected," expressed Sed, as he looked deeply into Marin's eyes.

Marin said, "I best turn the music way down or we may get into trouble."

Marin said while turning the sound system down, as if they were being recorded, "Sed, I have solved the sound system problem. We should have control of the sound system again," said Marin as she had a light shiver in her body and trembling in her eyebrows.

"Sed, maybe tomorrow we can walk through our neighborhood.

I really need a good walk after our rescue work at RenTahn. Oh, look out the window there, those flowers are just so magnificent. I need to just walk and smell the trees and flowers in our neighborhood Sed, in clear air, with you, Sed," said Marin, hugging Sed very tight and enjoying the view out of the window behind Sed. She thought quietly, "no bodies at last. I can't wait for the air to be clear, to be fresh again, to be normal."

The next morning Marin and Sed went out for a morning walk just as they used to for many years, holding hands and walking very close to each other. But the smiles of those past walks were gone as they strolled past their first neighbor and noticing the dead flowers where the husband and wife laid in the most savage, unjustified retaliation they had ever known.

"Sed, I have never heard of anything near what we are going through now, ever. I don't believe any of our paths have had a spiritual leader who is so strong willed, unwavering, and just dead set on being right about anything. I wonder how this all started, I don't get it," Marin said as she looked with love into her husband's eyes.

"Marin, you took the words right out of my mouth. Imagine declaring that your way is the only way. How she could take our capital and turn that into her temple center, that I will never understand.

It looks like a Guardian is moving in next door. Just what we don't need," stated Sed as they both observed a vehicle clearing out their neighbor's home and another vehicle behind which was delivering furniture for their new neighbor, a Guardian. Sed was thinking he never had a neighbor that he wouldn't like nor have any use for.

"Marin, my life since meeting you has opened like a flower, every day a fresh new blossom. You have flowered my life more than any dream ever has or ever will," stated Sed, kissing Marin on the side of her head.

"And now, Marin, I wonder what will unfold, day to day, sometimes even hour by hour," stated Sed as he and Marin walked through the neighborhood, quietly observing the many body silhouettes in the grass and flower beds of so many.

"Marin, I'm glad were' home. Those horrible body profiles on the lawns and flower beds will eventually disappear but sadly, I think they're stuck in my memory. they're With a Guardian moving in next door, and apparently a few more are moving into our neighborhood which means we must live under their idea of safety and security. What we had is gone and of that I'm so sorry Marin," said Neen as he sat down on the couch, caressing Marin.

"I hope you're all listening and recording everything, especially when we're in bed together in the evening. Are you also watching us? What kind of belief is this that you kill people over beliefs that are just different than yours or mine? Our neighborhood is gone and now our neighbor is a Guardian. Recording isn't enough. Now what?" yelled Marin in tearful anger. "Neen, I wonder if we will get a knock on the door after my tirade."

Neen replied "that he wouldn't be surprised at all. If anything happens to us, Marin, I wonder how Dad will be. Will QuaRen send her Guardians to RaedenOvul and then what.

I can't imagine Dad putting up with that QuaRen on his planet. No possible way."

After waiting for a few minutes for that expected knock on the door they got up and went into the kitchen to prepare dinner. Marin turned on the Viewer as it was time for the dinner broadcast of "the Evening Words of QuaRen".

Marin knew that regardless of what they might say here at home, they best turn on any scheduled broadcast of 'the QuaRen'.

The following morning Marin and Neen sat in their kitchen while enjoying the view of their many flowers out the picture window while savoring their most important morning coffee, the first cup always before breakfast.

"Neen," said Marin, "I must turn on the viewer in a few minutes but first let me pour some more coffee. I wish we could take off to RaedenOvul and spend some time with your dad. It's been so long since we have spent any time together."

Sed had placed two writing tablets on their table and handed one to Marin, stating that "sometimes I must take notes when I am with a patient and I find these new pads are excellent for my use," and immediately Sed handed a pad and pen to Marin.

Suddenly, Marin and Sed observed through their kitchen picture window, what appeared to be a large explosive flaming tongue coming down from the sky. That explosion created a strong vibration that shook throughout their home. Marin turned and grabbed Sed, kissing her husband lightly.

She said very quietly "Sed, do think if that so called QuaRen were killed that would end of this insanity?"

"I sure hope so, Marin. A revolution has begun. We must be successful. We have no choice," stated Sed at the lowest whisper he could.

It was time for QuaRens broadcast but oddly no broadcast came on. Perhaps the broadcast system had gone down temporarily. Sed actually hoped this QuaRen had been killed in the explosion.

A knock on the kitchen door and Marin answered, letting in, to her surprise and fear, Guardian Shawn, their new neighbor.

"Hello, you two, I'm the one who moved in next door, but I was ordered to do so, sorry. But that explosion was at the Interspace Construction Center. I expect the whole place is gone. The QuaRen was supposedly in the area for safety. If she was there, I doubt she would have survived that explosion."

"Well, I hope she did not survive. I want to be free again," stated Sed with great strength.

"I'm sorry, Sed and Marin, but it is my duty to declare you both traitors!" stated Guardian Shawn, like a military order.

Shawn took his pistol out of his holster and immediately shot both Marin and Neen, each in the heart.

RONSED PREPARES THE DEFENSE

onSed was checking on his planets defense system which had just passed the final necessary operational check.

RonSed had the hidden planetary defense system put into place shortly after the creation and rise of RenCeti and the QuaRen. After communicating with his son on the rising strength of the QuaRen he found this movement of RenCeti unacceptable. Discreetly RonSed had the components of a planetary defense system shifted from other destinations to RaedenOvul knowing that he would be the center of a successful revolution. A successful return to freedom, to normalcy, and to what he truly cherished, peace, tranquility, spiritual humility, and love. But truly, would anything be the same again. Yes, we can start afresh, the past may be gone but we haven't lost our inner strength, we haven't lost our true spirit.

RonSed had called for a meeting of his entire staff one week ago, set for today at three p.m., to discuss the latest he knew of in this rising underground revolution. They would meet in the auditorium. RonSed figured that this path would become more difficult as the actions of a few would bring disorder to this RenCeti on BathKohl and then to their other planets and colonies.

RonSed sat quietly, resting in meditative peace before the meeting, he reflected on his truth, he felt that he was only beginning to live. RonSed's childhood name was VonatSvaSed[15]. He remembered being the wanted light in his grandmothers' eyes.

RonSed, known as VonatSvaSed in his later teen years meet, dated, and married a beautiful girl, LynLinVonet[16].

LynLinVonet was the star, a sudden and totally unexpected joy. He remembered that day of quiet meditation at ShaneTahn when in a very peaceful state he raised his head, barely opening his eyes, he saw this woman opposite him, so beautiful. This was a moment that he never dreamed of this was just impossible, this wasn't him. Yet here he was, in love, really, was this honestly true or was this a timely moment to the opening of his heart in meditation, a lost moment of loneliness, a wondering for self, yet unresolved, perhaps unaccepted.

Their first date was at Sed's family home in WhazLin (translates as 'Daughter of the Tree'), close to Atom. His mother had never been happier in her life as when LynVonet accepted VonatSed and his family as hers to be from that moment forward.

The Sed family settled in Atum, losing their first born, a daughter. They're second born, a son, became NeenBonSed.

VonatSed began to dream of terraforming love in his teen years. In his teen years he was absent from home and his family for many hours at a time, delving into his terraforming studies.

VonatSed had to study the formation of a planet's atmosphere; the intended use of the planet would determine the atmosphere. Every major course of study in terraforming required on occasion an extended stay at another planet or a ship off the home world, BathKohl.

---

[15] VonatSvaSed: Sed being of the family Sed/Sva meaning son of Vonat. Vonat is his father's first name which translates as 'wonderer'.

[16] LynLinVonet - Monet being the family name/Lin meaning daughter/Lyn meaning female chef

In VonatSed's atmospheric studies he learned to determine that the intended purpose of the planet being terraformed would determine the atmosphere. If only acquiring a certain mineral was the purpose, what type of atmosphere was beneficial for mining. Part of that problem was the location of the planet from its sun(s), and should the orbit be left as it is or slightly altered for a cooling or warming benefit, or that perfect terraforming orbit that Earth science calls the "Goldilocks Orbit".

Then perhaps ultimate challenge, either disassembling a planet to reform it for the goal of oxygen-based life or terraforming it from the stage it was discovered in.

The next problem VonatSed had to solve was the issue of water. Did enough ice or liquid water exist for an oxygen-based planet. If it were an arid planet, would it be worth what it would take to develop water in the terraforming goal? Or just better to move further out into chartered or even unchartered regions of space in search for a better subject for terraforming.

RonSed was shaken from his dreamy memories by his assistant, Rhoz. "Ah yes, Rhoz, I was day-dreaming and must have lost track of time. It is time for me to get this meeting underway?"

As Rhoz began to answer RonSed, Rhoz looked away for a moment as tears began to swell in his eyes, "Ron, I am so sorry to have to tell you this, but your son and his wife have both been executed, apparently by a double-agent in the Guardian."

RonSed remained silent as his eyes glazed over for a few minutes. "Rhoz, thank you for your burden. I am shocked, but Rhoz I knew this would happen before we put an end to this RenCeti and that evil QuaRen. How can anyone call themselves spiritual when all other beliefs are illegal and punishable by death."

"RonSed, shall I cancel the meeting and let you have a quiet time for grieving?" asked Rhoz.

"No Rhoz. I thank you for carrying this loss, but I have no time to grieve right now, maybe never. We must make sure our defense systems are all manned and prepared for an attack from our home-world. Go ahead Rhoz and get the meeting started, I'll man-up and be along shortly," said RonSed with a cold stone face.

RonSed was shaken from his dreamy memories by his assistant, Rhoz. "Ah yes, Rhoz, I was day-dreaming and must have lost track of time. It is time for me to get this meeting underway?"

As Rhoz began to answer RonSed, Rhoz looked away for a moment as tears began to swell in his eyes, "Ron, I am so sorry to have to tell you this, but your son and his wife have both been executed, apparently by a double-agent in the Guardian."

RonSed remained silent as his eyes glazed over for a few minutes. "Rhoz, thank you for your burden. I am shocked, but Rhoz I knew this would happen before we put an end to this RenCeti and that evil QuaRen. How can anyone call themselves spiritual when all other beliefs are illegal and punishable by death."

"RonSed, shall I cancel the meeting and let you have a quiet time for grieving?" asked Rhoz.

"No Rhoz. I thank you for carrying this loss, but I have no time to grieve right now, maybe never. We must make sure our defense systems are all manned and prepared for a probably attack from our home-world. Go ahead Rhoz and get the meeting started, I'll man-up and be along shortly," said RonSed with a cold stone face.

RonSed sat in silence for a few minutes, totally lost from the presentation he would soon make. He tightened his eyes and held back his tears and thought to himself, "my son would want me to continue with what I am doing. He and Lyn both died for this revolution. Their service will be known in the future but to get there I must bring this revolution to triumph. How this all could have happened I will never understand but we must put an end it. Our original way of living will return regardless of the cost which will get higher I think, but I hope I am wrong.

"The auditorium was fully lit with a full house, as RonSed expected. "Thank you all for being here today. Our defense grid is up and running and from all the testing it is functioning at one hundred percent. And as you all probably know the RenCeti, and the Guardian are preparing to act for the worst possible, conceivable actions by order of the QuaRen. I know many have been murdered on BathKohl following the destruction of their temple. As I suspected would happen, RenCeti has secret operatives who are exposing some of our hidden operatives, with more success than I expected after the destruction of their temple, RenTahn.

Before I continue with this meeting, I am going to ask you all to join me for a few minutes in prayer and reflection for those we have lost and will lose.

Also, I must announce that I have lost my son NeenSed and his wife LynSed. They were both murdered in their home by a Guardian.

Ladies and Gentlemen, I could go on for some time about my loss but presently I think it is of greatest importance to make sure our defense systems are monitored and how that is to be handled is now to be presented by ClaironFon. ClaironFon, I turn the mike over to you. And thank you."

ClaironFon took the stage, thanking RonSed for his service and expressed her concern for the loss of his son and his son's wife. ClaironFon opened her presentation with "Ladies and Gentlemen, thank you for your patience for today's information on how our defense system is doing, especially about our security in this horrible, horrible time.

I am sorry that our original attempt to end this RenCeti and kill this QuaRen by blowing up that temple failed. Our second attempt also failed at the Interspace Construction Center, but she was wounded, and our intelligence says that unfortunately, she will recover.

Unfortunately, we expect our failure at the Center will bring more violent response and a probable attempt to bring QuaRen control of our planet. That we will never accept!"

The room rose in screams of "yes, yes, yes" while many expressed their anger while jumping and punching the air.

After those in the auditorium calmed down and returned to their seats, Clairon continued saying, "with the hard work of our community here on RaedenOvul we have created not only a great planet, but the greatest defense system ever built."

The auditorium filled with the bouncing echo of clapping hands of a vibrant celebration.

"Thank you, thank you. I know we are all honored and respected to each other in this community. And now, I will turn the mike over to RonSed, thank you all," said ClaironFon, bowing to the audience as she returned to her chair on the stage.

RonSed took the stage saying, "Again, welcome my fellow citizens of BathKohl, welcome to the beginning of our return!"

The auditorium sprang to great energy as all began saying, "BathKohl, BathKohl!" and then returned to their seats as RonSed motioned with his hands that all should return to their seats and sit down.

"My brothers and sisters," began RonSed, "with the dedication and work of so many in this room, we together have developed two new defensive systems which I will speak about now. In all our interspace history and interaction with other planets I have never seen nor heard of our first system which will go functional momentarily.

In the production of various parts of this defense shield the protective secrecy was necessary and worked. Not one person in the development of our defense system had information as to what they were constructing. They were making an item that belonged to something much larger. I had to do this to protect us and our goal from any possible double agent that might be among us.

Ladies and gentlemen, I am dropping the screen now and I want you to observe something in a moment. There, the screen is in place, and now, let me order Kron to activate the system. Kron, turn it on."

As everyone watched the screen showing their newly created home, RaedenOvul, in less than a minute RaedenOvul disappeared from the screen, only empty space could be seen.

In the same moment many in the auditorium said, "Wow, how did you do that?"

"My design, my ambition, my aspiration is what you have built which brought safety to RaedenOvul, and as you already knew, too some of our battleships. What you see on the screen is the true image of our location in space, now an apparent empty space. The image is from one of our defense crafts which was sent out of our orbit far enough for us to see this success. This system has no weapons, but with great care and silence we have acquired many of the best weapons available from BathKohl and other locations. I have named our defense system, "the BathKohl Defense System".

As I stated before many of us worked in great secrecy in the event there might be an active double agent amongst us, and that is why all off-planet communications have been down for a very long time, since before the temple destruction.

I won't take any questions on any information I have or will soon present. Questions will be meet in their due time and time will unveil itself when it is proper for me to do so, and I don't like that, but it is the only right answer. That is the trouble with freedom for me presently is that acceptance of responsibility if the best choice regardless of my discomfort with it. "Ok Kron," time to turn off the screen, said RonSed.

"And now I will make a presentation on our weaponized planetary defense system. I must tell you that all our interplanetary vessels have been armed to the fullest only due to the aid of those hidden in our freedom, our very own cloak of conspiracy.

Many of our ships have been weaponized to a point that I have classified a few of our vessels as Battle Ships. The Battleships ships have a new number of recently developed weapons. Several of our ships have our cloaking device, but I am not at liberty to name or in any way identify them. Those vessels also have a new system we call a Defensive Shield which will deflect shots from the weapons that we know of today. You may not communicate with anyone about this information unless I give you permission to do so. In the future we may have more to share but I can say that together our work will bring back our freedom of which this RenCeti robbed us. Let's get on with it!"

The auditorium sprang up shouting, hand clapping, and dancing.

As RonSed left the stage, he thought quietly to himself, "Devotion is the sacrifice that is the very loss of freedom and the surrender of responsibility, which has left us an unprecedented nightmare. This is what the QuaRen has brought us and yet she calls herself a spiritual leader, and as she claims, she is the leader of all. The very idea of power has never been part of our history but now this QuaRen walks in an illusion, the very illusion of power that her fallacy has created with her very, very dark heart. How could we possible have ended up where we are at."

As everyone left the auditorium, they walked past tables with each having a stationed armed guard. That guard handed out the new assignments, each being in a security sealed envelope with each person's name printed on it.

CHAPTER 11

"RIGHTEOUS CONTROL IS FREEDOM"

"Ladies and Gentlemen, my fellow children of Ren, we are gathered here today, in a time when we are in the rapids of our waters flow. Today we are taking time together, and that time together is in a unified reflection which is gathering strength in our freedom while we celebrate acceptance in the water of our life. Sadly, after all this time many here on BathKohl and our sister planets, many are staying willingly in murky, pooling, stinking, shallow waters where in I see a debris of sadness and the very rot of sin. I see the flow of life is lost amongst many who are drowning in their misinterpretation of our spiritual path and in others, an absolute denial of the only true spiritual path. They are unable to flow with us in the truth, the Ren. Those outside of our Ren are bewildered and yet must be saved. We have spent much time in patience.

It is a sin that we must live in fear, we who flow in the water. We join here today in the beauty of our rebuilt temple, and we celebrate the completion of repairs at our Interspace Construction Center. Why anyone would want your QuaRen dead or to even damage our temple is beyond my understanding, especially since I bring to all the only spiritual truth through which the Ren blesses all our lives.

I bring a gift of escape for those who have not joined our path, our stream. At the opening of this service our Guardians here on BathKohl have begun to release those who stay upon the shoals and refuse our Ren. I have also ordered our Guardians to take this blessed gift of Ren to our terraformed planets. First blessings are presently on their way to RaedenOvul where AhbendRaRonSed and our best scientists all reside, expanding the playground of our souls.

As the hall grew quiet apprehension could be felt throughout the temple. Although the weather was sunny and clear there was a great darkness spreading over BathKohl.

The QuaRen rose raised her arms while looking about the hall, "My sisters and brothers, I love you truly as my sisters and brothers. While we leave our temple, Ren, I can tell you that we always have our temple within us no matter where we are, alone or with another of our family."

CHAPTER 12

"DEFENSE, THE BATTLE FOR FREEDOM"

"Kron, at last we have a few moments together, alone at last. While I don't know what will happen next, but with you my love, I will make it through," said RonSed to Kron as they hugged in a gentle kissing embrace.

"RonSed, I see you as everyone's grandfather and I love you more than anyone. My life has never been so fulfilled since I married you," said Kron to RonSed.

There was a sudden strong knock on the door and ClaironFon entered, "excuse me RonSed and Kron but our outer defense ships have detected the approach of a number of war ships and our intelligence says that the QuaRen has ordered a number of war ships to come here and fulfill her goal. She wants control of all terraformed planets, you and your team. I knew this was coming but this is much sooner than I expected," stated ClaironFon. The three joined in hands for a few moment

"Well, let's get on with it. ClaironFon, please order all systems to war alert and order all ships to cloak. Our planetary cloak is already on so maybe they won't see RaedenOvul, thinking that something went wrong with our terraforming and were all gone. If any ship comes into our atmosphere with a trajectory online with our living center take them out and no warning, obliterate them. And tell all our ships not to fire unless they're in our atmosphere, otherwise wait for my orders."

"Yes Sir, RonSed," stated ClaironFon as she exited their residence.

RonSed and Kron ran out of their residence in a rush to the defense headquarters. They both stopped for a minute while looking into each other's eyes just outside the doors expressing great concern.

"Kron, how are the readings on the energy level for our planets shield?" asked RonSed.

"There at 100% Ron. Shall we turn the system on?" asked Kron to RonSed.

"Let's double check that all vessels with shields have them on. Next, I want their lead ship to attempt communication with the approaching Ren ships but keep those shields up. If they respond tell them to turn around and return to BathKohl. If they don't reply or refuse to turn around then at that point, warn them they have two minutes to abort their mission or they will be fired upon. Kron, tell our ships to take out those Ren ship engines if possible. Destroy any ship only as deemed necessary. Tell them what I said are orders and that unfortunately this could be the opening of an all-out war which we will win!"

While Kron informed their defense ships to prepare for battle, RonSed made an announcement over the planets emergency communication system of the expected attack from the Ren Guardians of BathKohl and that they were now on a war footing. RonSed was now ordering the planets defense system into full operation.

"RonSed calling Alonfen[17], come in Alonfen."

"Commander LynLouOn of the Alonfen here, RonSed."

"Lyn, I'm so glad you're there. How does RaedenOvul look on your system?"

---

[17] Alonfen translates in English as 'first Explorer'

"Ron, wow, it's working perfectly. She's gone, absolutely gone. It works RonSed, it works."

"Great, Lyn, were at step one with success in our defense.

Now, if you can run a test and let me know if our cloaked warships are working well. Order all ships, cloaked or not, to use our priority scramble in all communications until I order otherwise and use the re-routed com system. Absolutely no direct communication to our base."

"I will check it out and make sure all ships are using our priority scramble and get back to you RonSed as soon as I can confirm our cloaking is working."

"Ok Lyn, I will be right here waiting for your confirmation. Out."

The ship Alonfen, while transmitting security orders to all their ships went into high alert status. The ship was already cloaked when the ship automatically sounded the alert. The Alonfen bridge staff found three ships from Bathkohl entering the defense area of the Alonfen.

"This is Commander LynLouOn of the RaedenOvul war ship Alonfen, I need to know what you three ships are doing. We know you are war ships."

"This is Guardian Commander Toner. I cannot find your ships on any of our instruments. Have you a need for our help?"

"No commander Toner, we are near you and none of your efforts will see our ship. We order you to turn around and return to BathKhol or surrender your ship immediately." "This is Commander Toner and I want to know why you're challenging the will of our QuaRen. She brings peace to you all and asks us to bring the Word of Ren to all on the planet RaedenOvul."

"Commander Toner, our purpose is to return BathKohl and our entire planetary system to the freedom that all of lost with this Ren and your priestess, QuaRen.

We grant you have the freedom of your religious or spiritual path, but not at the cost of freedom, the cost of personal choice, or the cost of our history for the limited view of one person.

Commander Toner, your' ordered to leave this space immediately or surrender your ships. You have five minutes to surrender or leave. If you have not done so, then in five minute's we will destroy your three ships. This communication is terminated for that five minute."

"The five minutes I gave you has passed Commander Toner, what is your reply?" asked Commander LynLouOn. Sir, you must reply now, or we will fire upon your ships."

"RonSed, Commander LynLouOn here. The three ships have not replied within our five-minute demand. Shall we fire to disable engines or take them out?"

"RonSed here Commander Lyn. If possible, take out their engines first. If they fire any weapons, then respond as you deem necessary. Keep me informed."

The three warships under the command of RonSed pulled back from the three ships of the Ren for their own safety. Should they have to destroy these three ships they were ready.

After a safe distance the three warships of RaedenOvul fired upon the three enemy vessels, taking out their engines

With the security scramble for their communications, Commander LynLouOn sent a message to their other two warships that they were to move after every weapon's firing as there may be a traceable path which could present a targeting moment.

Commander LynLouOn called Commander Toner, "Commander Toner, would you please surrender you ships to us after which we will board and disarm each vessel. Upon surrender Commander Toner we will guarantee your crews safety. Any firing upon as even though you cannot find us, will result in complete destruction of any ship firing."

Kron at that moment opened a communication to Commander LynLouOn, "Kron here commander, RonSed will be here in a moment, and here he is commander." "Commander, what is happening?" asked RonSed.

"RonSed, three ships sit ready to fire. I ordered them to surrender after we took out their engines. They refuse to communicate and have been warned we will take them out if they activate their weapons. Oh no, they're activating their weapons," stated Commander LynLouOn.

"Commander Toner, Commander LynLouOn here. Do not charge your weapons. If you fire your weapons our response will be total. Am I understood Commander?"

The three BathKohl warships starting firing in an apparently programmed pattern.

Commander LynLouOn ordered her ships to fire with total strength at the three BathKohl warships. Within moments the three aggressive warships were destroyed with no survivors.

Commander LynLouOn gave an order to her ships that "if any surviving escape capsules are found bring them in while locking those vessels at a safe distance, then scan them for any type of weapons or any form of explosive device. Place any survivors in the brig. Make sure medical care is given as needed and they are allowed no communication.

Absolutely no communications by any survivor on any ship and that is a Direct Order. They are prisoners of war, and I will determine any rights. Over and out."

Commander LynLouOn sat quietly on her bridge as her crew used everything they had in search for survivors.

"Lieutenant Jon, have you found any possible survivors?" asked Commander LynLouOn as she was looking at their main screen on the bridge with very wet eyes.

"Sorry Commander, but a thorough search has only recognized debris. Communications through our system and from those of the DonRigger and the RahPrize have found no evidence of any survivors."

"Thank you, Char. Please hail RonSed and I'll take the call here," stated Commander LynLouOn.

A few minutes later Commander LynLouOn received a call, "RonSed here Commander."

Commander LynLouOn replied, "I am sad to inform you RonSed that we had to take out all three of the Guardian vessels. Our warning apparently wasn't considered serious as in minutes all three of the Guardian warships began a random firing pattern obviously hoping to hit our ships. I ordered a return at full strength, and we took out the three ships. Our search has concluded that there are no survivors RonSed."

"Sorry to hear that Commander. We need all ships to stay on alert and if you feel safe take down your shields. All communications are to remain coded. If any one of our ships finds one of theirs on scope they are to cloak immediately and notify me as soon as it is safe to do so." All ships are to order any approaching ship from BathKohl to surrender whether they are a military vessel or civilian, and if their response is not considered honest, if it appears safe, disable them and when in doubt use a full response and take out that ship. No captured ships or crew are to be brought near RaedenOvul nor any communication between our crew members excluding medical aid. Absolutely no conversations. We are in a state of war now Commander, so our first response is to win in any situation. I will attempt to contact RenCeti on BathKohl and that QuaRen and I will ask if they step down from this war. Keep me informed. RonSed over and out."

CHAPTER 13

"LET US END THE FREETHINKER. THE QUAREN"

"Ah, Guardian SironLashval, please come in. I was just considering calling you to ask how our mission to RaedenOvul has gone. Hopefully they have converted as their gift of terraforming is certainly a gift from the Ren."

"I'm sorry QuaRen but the news is not as hoped for," replied SironLashval.

QuaRen answered, "I suppose they want to stay out of our Ren, our path. Perhaps they are confused and holding the keys to terraforming they believe they can stay in a secondary stream or on shore from our Ren. Those former paths are all mirrors of shadows of pathways that lead away from our truth. So, my Guardian what is our problem with our AhbendRaRonSed?"

"QuaRen, our three battleships that were assigned to RaedenOvul were all destroyed and to our present knowledge there are no survivors," said SironLashval while standing more at attention than was necessary for his Guardian ranking.

"What?" replied the QuaRen as she stood up behind her office desk with both hands in fists of rage hitting upon her desk. Suddenly she with her tight fists she threw everything off her desk as she screamed in great anger, using words unknown to the Guardian who stepped back from the desk, trembling from her rage.

A Guardian opened the door and asked if there was need of help and the QuaRen answered, "my apologies Guardian for my rare and unusual anger. I apologize and ask you both for forgiveness."

"No problem my QuaRen. With your word I will close the door and forget this moment," stated Guardian SironLashval.

"Yes, everything is ok. And thank you Guardian. Please close the door. I shall try not to get lost in my emotions again," stated the QuaRen with a definite look of rage in her eyes as she slowly let her hands relax after expressing her physical anger.

"There is more my QuaRen. The information we received from the ships is that they had a challenge to surrender as they approached RaedenOvul, but no ships could be found on the scopes. What is strange is that there was no reading of RaedenOvul on any of our ship's instruments. We have that in our tracking records of all three ships and there is no equipment failure, especially on our three ships at the same time. I could find nothing in our information systems to explain this occurrence. At present our scientists are completely baffled," said Guardian SironLashval.

The entry door opened, and Guardian Renwa entered saluting the QuaRen. "Guardian, how can I help you?" asked the QuaRen.

"QuaRen, we have a message from Sed of RaedenOvul."

"What is it Guardian," stated QuaRen harshly and showing rising anger.

"You are asked to step down from any war actions and to enter negotiations."

"Negotiations, from what. Guardian, do we have a communication link to Sed?" "Yes QuaRen, a direct link as I understand it."

"Thank you, Guardian, you may return to your position."

QuaRen met that evening with her terraforming crew, all students of AhbendRaRonSed, now serving the QuaRen. No member of the Ren Terraforming crew had any idea what could have happened to Sed's planet, RaedenOvul, nor how their battleships were engaged and destroyed by ships that did not show on any visual screens. After much discussion and exchange of ideas, it was decided by the QuaRen that this terraforming science crew should be the communicators with Sed and by the guidance of the QuaRen, work on Sed and his scientists of RaedenOvul, to convert them into the stream of Ren.

C H A P T E R 14

"A N I M P O S S I B L E D R E A M"

"**K**ron, I see so many of us sleep-walking into a growing nightmare, a nightmare I simply cannot imagine. Many days may pass, Kron, before we will have such a loving private time together again. I hope that I can say over and over again my greatest truth, I love you Kron and I always will, always, always."

"And I will always love you Sed no matter what. I don't think it will be long before we hear from the Guardians," stated Kron as he held Sed close to him on their bed.

"Why do you say the Guardians Kron?" asked Sed with a little surprise on his face.

"Sed, I think that the QuaRen will not talk to us directly but instead will have someone high up her Guardians represent her in any negotiations. I personally think no matter what she says she can't be trusted. She is addicted to this false idea of personal power and control which I see her expressing through this Ren. So Sed, don't trust anything she says," said Kron, and then gently kissed Sed's forehead.

A couple of hours later a gentle knock was on their door, leading Kron to say, "It's a good thing we got the good sleep we did as I think that gentle knock on our door is our last restful sleep for a long time, for us and everyone. No matter how this turns out Sed I will love you more tomorrow than today. I am always with you," said Kron.

"A knock on the door, I didn't hear that at all," said Sed as he touched the door button. "All right, come in, come in," stated Sed very gently as he slid off the bed, slowly sliding his right hand across Kron's neck.

"Sorry to disturb you two but we do have an incoming message from QuaRen. We received an initial message from a Guardian RenWa giving us a test for communications and then stating that a message from QuaRen would be sent within the hour. I believe our cloaking has them quite confused," said ClairOn.

"Thank you ClairOn. We will be in the control room in a few minutes." After ClairOn left their quarters, Sed, looking at Kron with a serious look on his face, said, "Now let's work on the impossible dream of bringing back our culture and most of all, our individual freedom."

The control room was full of every station manned as Kron and Sed entered.

"Listen everyone, we will have to pay attention to all communications from BathKohl and any foreign ship near any of our terraformed planets and our ships. And bounce all our communications off any local satellites to hide our location. Ok, what do we know?" asked Sed.

"A communication is coming in, Sed, from RenCeti. Do you want it at your station or on the com?"

"Put it on the com. I want everyone to listen so if I need your advice, it will be right there," stated Sed.

"This is Guardian SironLashval of RenCeti. I cannot confirm the goal of my communication being RaedenOvul as we can find no evidence of planet RaedenOvul on our scopes. I have been asked to communicate with AhbendRaRonSed as I am representing and speaking for 'the QuaRen' of our RenCeti." "AhbendRaRonSed here and open to communication, and please call me Sed."

"Hello Sed. 'The QuaRen' sends her best. My first question is where you are and what happened to your terraformed planet, RaedenOvul. I am sending this communication to the location of RaedenOvul on our star-map and I am wondering how is our communication's reception; and is your planet gone?" asked the Guardian.

"Lashval, I'm not answering your questions. What do you have to say from your QuaRen?" stated Sed.

"What do you mean 'you're QuaRen', she is of the Ren for all of us," said Lashval with a voice shaking with some fear.

"Lashval, we will bring back the culture we had before this QuaRen, with respect and freedom as we have always lived with in our society. The Ren and your QuaRen may continue but only as a spiritual group living in total respect for the path of another. Judgement is not welcomed. The Guardian and 'the QuaRen' must end all military action immediately and live-in total acceptance of all others and their personal spiritual path," said Sed, shaking his head while looking down at his desktop and tightly gripping the back of his chair.

"Sed, 'the QuaRen' asks that you and your team enter into the Ren and receive the blessings of 'the QuaRen'. She says that she is to bring the word of RenCeti to all," stated Guardian Lashval.

"Lashval, you must inform your QuaRen that this RenCeti may not continue in its horrid abuse of the path of others.

This murder stops right now, and she and the Guardian must surrender to RaedenOvul immediately. We consider ourselves to be in a state of war with the RenCeti. Believe me Lashval, we will use our weapons to achieve our goal which is to return to the freedom of one's own path as it was on BathKohl in all our history, before you. Your RenCeti is the opposite of love. RenCeti is the opposite of acceptance and humility, and you are everything that we are not. We give your QuaRen one day to surrender. Send your communication the same as you have done today. End of transmission Lashval." "What!" yelled Lashval.

C H A P T E R 15

"TAKE OUT THE HARBOR"

"QuaRen, Sed has declared war and stated that you and RenCeti may continue if we return to the society of BathKohl as it was before Ren. The spiritual paths chosen by anyone must be respected or this war will continue until RenCeti is history," reported Lashval to 'the QuaRen' while looking directly at her with light tears shedding from his eyes while attempting to hide his sorrow although it was slipping out in his voice.

The QuaRen replied, "I am deeply saddened Guardian Lashval that Sed and his followers refuse to join us in the Ren.

Lashval, they are like ocean water lapping against the hull of their boat and that boat is grounded upon a beach, a beach lost from the flowing waters of our Ren. Repairs of their boat will be of no use as their word for acceptance is but a stench of rotting bodies. We must remove that stranded hull from that shore.

How many battle cruisers can we use against Sed on our RaedenOvul?"

"I do not know QuaRen, I will have to ask our Defense Council," answered the Guardian Lashval.

A few hours later Guardian Lashval returned to 'the QuaRen' with the Cruiser information.

"My QuaRen, the Defense Council is uncertain on your request. Their search has no image from any of our sources of the planet RaedenOvul nor have they been able to locate any of Sed's war ships. They suggest we do more research into our inability to locate any of their warships and ultimately, what has happened to planet, RaedenOvul. They remind us that we lost all of our warships that you ordered to RaedenOvul, and they believe at present we could lose all vessels sent into that area," stated the Guardian Lashval.

"Their advice is wise Guardian Lashval. Let research continue to what has happened to RaedenOvul and how we lost our ships. Let's have our Defense Council ask our trading partners for any information that can aid us in this problem and hopefully get any useful information to me as quickly as possible," stated Guardian Lashval as he slowly exited from the QuaRen's office, bowing his head towards the QuaRen.

The QuaRen sat in her office, alone in guarded silence as she waited for a useful answer to her needs. In quiet reflection she knew the RenCeti must continue, that we must move on to our terraformed planets, and then to the many others. Flowing in the Ren has no judgement of a planet or of a species. All must be in the flow of the Ren or be released from the shoals of their lives so that they may join me in the Ren, the one and only truth of the Spirit.

A hard knock on her door brought the QuaRen's attention to her office door, "Good to see you Guardian Lashval. Tell me, what has our Defense Committee figured out?"

"My QuaRen, they have found no answers, no information to any of our inquiries from anyone, from any traders or any type of ship from any planet. At present no one understands how our Warships found no screen images in their opening battle with Sed's ships. Our ships should have seen the planet RaedenOvul, its size could not have been missed on any search. The committee has searched for RaedenOvul, and several our trading planets also searched from your request and detected only empty space where RaedenOvul should be in its orbit.

No one received a response from any communications sent to RaedenOvul. The Defense Committee recommended that we send two research vessels and four battle-cruisers to our mapped location of RaedenOvul in full war mode. They suggested that outside the zone where we lost our ships, communications be opened to Sed while having all ships prepared to track the origin of any communications from Sed. With your approval, as soon as the location source of the signals are centered, we immediately fire torpedoes to that target site, possibly taking out Sed and bring this problem to a close," said Guardian Lashval while standing at military ease.

"I give permission for such a military response. Keep me informed when facts are known, not guesses or hopes," responded 'the QuaRen' as she stood, turning her back to the Guardian who then exited.

CHAPTER 16

BATTLEFIELD

Kron gently woke Sed, "Sed, there has been a continuing signal attempting to connect with us from the military center on BathKohl. I decided that before any contact is accepted, I needed to alert you to this." "Any information in the signal?"

Kron replied "that our tracking crew said this signal seems to have only a locating ping in it," ClairOn opened the front door to their quarters and asked if it was okay to enter "Come in ClairOn, were in the front room".

"Sed, I ordered one of our ships to analyze this signal before we respond to it and the ships analysis revealed that it contains a location program search. It appears to be a target search aimed at our center here on RaedenOvul, undoubtedly by order of the QuaRen. Figuring the distance involved they will have planned a weapon's launch from the military center on BathKohl and my guess is they will use interplanetary defense torpedoes. Most likely if they get an answer then they will have this center located and launch an immediate attack.

"ClairOn, how long has the message been beaming at us?" asked Sed.

"Our reception has been for thirty-five minutes. The team would like your decision on our next choice hoping we still have an active signal," stated ClairOn.

The three headed to the control center, immediately walking over to the main viewing screen which displayed the incoming signal while observing their cruiser that scattered the signal while displaying on a side screen the origin of the signal.

The entire crew stood near the two screens and were looking at Sed while waiting for a decision from him. "Everyone, I need your immediate suggestions on this problem," Sed stated expressing his concern while looking across the room at everyone.

"Sed, I want the Commander LynLouOn of our battleship Alonfen deflecting this signal online and communicate with me right now, ok?" asked ClairOn.

Commander LynLouOn joined communication with Sed immediately.

There was no doubt that the QuaRen was attempting to target the science center on RaedenOvul.

Sed's forehead became a wrinkled graveled road while he stood unusually straight and tall as he said to everyone," In my opinion we are left with no choice but to give a military response. I have no doubt that the QuaRen was wanting to acquire communication with the only true purpose to target and kill us all. I now order that we fire missiles targeting the origin of this signal and I want total destruction of that site. But, as suggested, no missiles fired at that RenTahn Temple for it really is our capitol, NorisColren of BathKohl. Commander, fire everything it takes at your judgement to take out that base. Fire immediately if you can Commander before we lose her signal which will target our torpedoes to that base."

The QuaRen was in the temple trying to relax through meditation as Guardian SironLashval quietly entered the temple and stood observing from the top row of the auditorium seats. He looked around the inner temple where meditation and The Guardian quietly wondered if this path was truly correct or is this just a bad time in the foundation of this RenCeti. His hands grasped the rail in front of him as anger and fear seemed to mix silently within him.

Suddenly the ground shook violently and numerous loud explosions could be heard echoing inside the temple. After the shaking and thunderous sound stopped the Guardian received a call on his phone.

While the Guardian was running down the steps toward the QuaRen he yelled, "QuaRen, I am sorry to interrupt your meditation, but I have very bad news to tell you."

The QuaRen got up slowly and turned to the Guardian SironLashval, looking him directly in his eyes, "You have information already on what the shaking and what those thunderous rumbles are from?"

"I am sorry to report to you, my QuaRen, that our primary defense base has been totally destroyed. Our secondary defense headquarters said there was a tracking on our communications to Sed's science center. It is too early to know if there are any survivors at our base, but I have been informed that the blast area extends far beyond the borders of the base," said the Guardian Lashval.

"No, no, no!" screamed the QuaRen while throwing a glass towards the Guardian.

"I can't believe this. I never thought that in the Ren such a nightmare would happen, especially near our RenTahn. No meditation ever showed me such a horror. Perhaps war is the word, a word I never thought I would use.

Have our Military Council convene here immediately on what we are capable of in response to this attack.

The QuaRen cleaned up the broken glass that she had thrown at SironLashval which hit near the main door and scattered. Then she stood in a trance while apparently looking out her window at the smoke billowing across the valley. She never dreamed that in ordering the tracking of her signal would bring just the opposite of her command. How can anyone attack me and the Ren that I speak for. My calling has never had an image of war in any meditation. I just don't get this, but I have no choice. I want Sed's base taken out and Sed with it! Perhaps terraforming is the issue. Could it be that it is something we chose which we were never to do in the flow of the Ren.

A heavy knock woke her out of her stupor, "If that is you Guardian Lashval, please enter."

"QuaRen, I'm sorry for the time it took but the Military Council is here. May we enter," asked Guardian Lashval.

Tears and anger were obvious on QuaRen's face as she turned toward her Military Council in the conference chamber.

"Council, I want to hear what you have to say about this attack on our main military base," said the QuaRen in an unusually deep voice for her.

"QuaRen, our base was one-hundred percent destroyed and there are no survivors. We think that many residents near the base were killed as the explosions went wider than the base perimeter, but we haven't had the time to ascertain the complete extent of damage outside the base," stated the Commander in a somewhat sweaty face and a shaken voice. "Commander, this is something I never expected," said the QuaRen.

"Neither did we QuaRen. In following our orders no one thought of this possible action in our plan to take out Sed's base, no one," stated the Commander. "We received no signal in return from Sed and before we gave up on our communication to Sed, our base had been hit.

We think our base was hit by the same type of torpedoes that we intended to launch on Sed's base. It was one instantaneous multi warhead hit. Not expecting such an attack as being possible at all, we were not looking with our defense system for any attack," explained the Commander.

"Commander, do you know if our Defense Committee has a plan to take out Sed after this attack. I want Sed found, and I want to know what happened to planet RaedenOvul and if RaedenOvul has broken up why haven't I been told about a ton of debris in that orbit. Why haven't you located any of the battle cruisers assigned to our three terraformed planets," stated the QuaRen, hitting the table hard with her right fist, shaking the entire table.

It was obvious that everyone sitting at the table was shook-up when the QuaRen hit the table as hard as she did and then she placed both her arms on the table intently looked around at each seated person with harsh discomforting eye- contact.

After a few moments of intolerable stillness in the room the Commander began to speak from his seat, "QuaRen, I apologize for any questions that have not been answered but these questions are extremely difficult to resolve."

"I will turn this problem of RaedenOvul's disappearance over to our Chief Security Officer, Lieutenant RonLi," stated the Commander as he nodded to his Lieutenant.

"QuaRen, our best scientists believe that Sed and his terraforming crew have developed some type of defense system that cloaks a planet and his battleships from any type of detection, visual or instrumental. As to your statement about any debris in RaedenOvul's orbit absolutely no debris has been detected and if the planet was destroyed there would have to be some debris in that orbit. Since there is none, our conclusion is that RaedenOvul is in its orbit. We have enough history on RaedenOvul that we have been able to compute its orbit and knowing the location of Seds base, we can launch an attack at your command, my QuaRen," informed the Lieutenant to all present.

The QuaRen asked directly with her eyes on the Lieutenant, "Lieutenant, can we find any ships under Seds command?"

"Not from our present understanding QuaRen. Unless a ship becomes visible, we have no present ability to locate it and even if we find a hidden ship it could move before we could target it," replied the Lieutenant.

"Commander, do your best to find a way to target Sed's battleships but if you can communicate before firing, ask them to immediately surrender and remain visible. After you board those ships and take control on the main deck place their commander and staff into the smallest security quarters on the ship and with the least comforts possible. I order you to use the information you have and launch an attack on Sed's home-base as soon as possible. Keep this information quiet Commander with only those in the need to know," stated the QuaRen.

C H A P T E R 17

"EVACUATE"

"Thank-you everyone for being on time. I have been thinking of what I would do if I were in the QuaRen's shoes, and I am sure she would launch a counter strike to our base as quickly as possible. Her military science crew could figure out our orbit from all the information in their system and if I were them, I would compute the orbital location of RaedenOvul and do a torpedo launch to this target. I believe we must evacuate immediately and that is my direct order. I have already contacted two battleships and they are in orbit and waiting for us. I will leave our defense system on. Follow our practice drills from our terraforming work so let's go right now," Sed firmly voiced to his terraforming staff and then he turned to the emergency exit corridor and headed to the Battleship Alonfen.

When Sed's battleships were passing RaedenOvul's moon, Onvus, Sed and his staff were observing their science center on various screens when suddenly, but expectedly, explosions lite up the screens. Their base had become a fireball as it evaporated into history before their eyes.

"Sed, now what do we do," Kron asked while hugging Sed and shedding a few tears, "where do we go now Sed."

Both battleships, the Alonfen and RaunLee, halted on the far side of their moon, Onvus.

"Commander, please open our communications with both ships but use a tight signal that will not go further out than between us," requested Sed of Commander LynLouOn on the deck of the Alonfen.

A few minutes later the staff of both ships were in silence as they waited for Sed's announcement.

"Ladies and gentlemen, Sed here. First, I want to express my thanks to the staff of both ships and my gratitude that we are all alive. Thank you for such accurate response on our emergency evacuation procedures.

As you all know, we have lost our base within the last hour. I turned off our shield on RaedenOvul directly following QuaRen's hit on our base hoping that she and her Guardians believe that they have taken us out.

Myself and our two ship Commanders, ClairOn and LynLouOn have kept an important secret that only now in this unfortunate circumstance will I reveal. As you know the slow rotation and orbit of our moon keeps the other side permanently facing BathKohl. We have constructed an outpost here on the dark side which is buried and that includes our ship landing facilities. Now, on both ships the Lieutenants will hand out a brief to everyone. Those briefs contain all the information to introduce you to this base which will include your housing which has been pre-assigned, the lab facilities, all dinning and social areas and activities available. After we get settled, we will have an evening meal together in the main dining hall and our ship commanders will instruct us on our defensive systems.

Immediately following dinner, there will be a period for questions. Barring any emergency, we will take tomorrow off and get settled and if you want another day, please let me know as your individual communicators have a message number for me. And now, Commanders, take us in to our new home." Sed and Kron sat down together on the steps, each resting an arm on the others shoulder.

CHAPTER 18

THE HIDDEN SETTLEMENT

The organized commotion began to settle about breakfast time of the first morning on the moon Onvus. Most did not have any sleep that night but at breakfast time everyone headed to the community dining room. The staff was amazed upon entering the dining room for breakfast and that breakfast was already prepared and available in a great looking buffet line. Apparently, a staff was on site and already in service.

Many of the staff took two mugs of coffee to their tables and saluted the cooking staff with a coffee mug in appreciation for such unexpected service. There was enough food prepared for a second serving by most to the buffet line.

Sed and Kron were also in the dining room and after the second serving of breakfast, Sed rose up and asked for everyone's attention;

"First, let us all take a few moments in silent reflection, giving thanks for our success and safety, and in memory of those lost in this war. Also, I want to thank Kron for being with me through this as without him I don't see how I could have gotten through it all."

A great applause filled the room expressing everyone's appreciation for the work of Sed and Kron who both stood in great surprise. During the applause they both turned around where they stood in the cafeteria, waving a thank you too all.

"Thank you, everyone. My husband and I are greatly surprised, and we thank you all," said Sed as he kept standing while Kron took his seat. "I am amazed and very thankful that we are all alive and safe here at our hidden base. I heard someone suggest that we name our base, 'The Hidden Settlement', and if you all agree, let's do it," stated Sed while smiling at everyone as they clapped in approval of the base name.

Sed began speaking, "We may be isolated, but we are free and alive. When I began in my research which has, with your help, led to our successful terraforming, I couldn't help moving to our first successful planet. There certainly may have been unknown dangers but our apparent success couldn't be stopped by doubt or fear. And now the success of many, many years of mutual respect and social acceptance has been erased by the strangest belief our home planet has ever known. I want our home, BathKohl, to return to the love and acceptance that is our life.

I have always thought of our battleships as a last defense against the unknown and never, never dreamed, that we would use our weapons and ships against our own people, but we have no choice, none, none at all.

Thankfully we have this base which is well hidden. It will take us a week or more to get settled in and at the same time we will have some computations to review. When we communicate with the QuaRen, our ships will go to a prechosen co-ordinate before searching for incoming communications or communicating with one of our other bases. I say to our ship commanders that if you don't feel safe communicating to anyone, then don't do it.

ClairOn can't be here right now but that quiet woman set up our communication procedure which should continue to hide our base.

Before I make any further military response to the QuaRen and her Guardians I will first share ideas with our commanders. I have a final choice weapon hidden well which I will not discuss at this time, but I will keep quiet about until we are so damaged that I see no other choice.

As for now you are all welcome to explore our new base. Tomorrow at 0800 please be at your assigned stations so you can become familiar with this new location. Your posts and duties are the same and all updated information will be at everyone's post. If there are any immediate duty changes, I believe ClairOn will discuss that with everyone that may have a change of duty. I don't know about you, but I need another mug of Java and another round of breakfast.

In a moment I will sit down and shut up but first let us all thank this wonderful kitchen staff," stated Sed as he sat down at his table.

Everyone stood up in the cafeteria, clapping and hooting loudly in appreciation of the kitchen staff and then everyone headed back in line for another round of breakfast.

The following morning, just before 8 a.m., Kron and Sed were on the base command deck which looked just like a battlecruiser command deck.

Sed sat back at his post for a few minutes enjoying the calming silence that surrounded him and then he stood-up, looking at everyone, saying, "I am going to open a communication to the QuaRen and by ClairOn's work, there will be no way that her Guardians or anyone will be able to track our signal to any viable origin. I am hoping to talk to her directly and I will allow this conversation to go over our intercom system, but I am asking everyone to remain silent until I say otherwise."

ClairOn notified Sed that communication with the QuaRen was established and turned the system over to his desk.

"Hello QuaRen, this is Sed of the terraforming team. If our communication is stable, then we can discuss our issues on what has recently happened between us."

"Hello Sed, QuaRen here. I am surprised to hear from you as I figured that hit on your base at RaedenOvul probably killed you. I am surprised and thankful to hear you Sed. I guess you were not at that post when it was taken out by those devastating weapons hit."

"Right QuaRen, I was off the planet when my base was hit and totally wiped out. My guess is that you ordered a hit on our base from your Guardians due to the growing chasm between us. Am I not, correct?" asked Sed.

"Hi Sed, I really do not know who attacked you and I don't understand it at all.

I was thinking during this conversation that we should track the origin of your signal and send a ship out to rescue you if that is needed but my Guardian says they can't seem to locate a source. If you can tell me where you're at I can send a rescue ship for you Sed," stated the QuaRen.

"Would you fire a weapon at me QuaRen. Isn't that really why you want to know where I am?" asked Sed. "Sed, how you think that of me, your QuaRen."

"QuaRen, as far as I am concerned, we are all equal and nothing more. I have interest in this nightmare you have created, this RenCeti, a nightmare, a total nightmare," stated Sed as his face grimaced in anger.

The QuaRen began yelling her response to Sed, "Damn it Sed, you have caused this waring breakdown of our society, not me, your QuaRen Sed, your QuaRen!".

"Your' no one's QuaRen. It is time to put an end to this "my way or you have no way". How can you believe you have the only valid path on BathKohl, you're the only one who knows it all? Since I won't pay the toll on your bridge you would kill me, isn't that, right?" asked Sed.

"Sed, I have no choice, I must follow my instructions in the bringing of RenCeti to our BathKohl. You and everyone actively working with you on terraforming must immediately join into the flow of the Ren or I must hunt you down and free every one of you," said the QuaRen.

"ClairOn, cut this communication off right now!" ordered Sed, and it was cut off immediately.

"Thanks to everyone here for being quiet through this discussion with QuaRen. Now I think we should all get to our duties and as important information becomes available I or someone will make an announcement," stated Sed as he, Kron, and ClairOn headed to their side office.

"Wow," stated Sed as the three of them entered their side office, "now we definitely have a headache. What advice do you have through our ship commanders ClairOn? I believe achieving peace is not going to be an easy walk."

"Well look at that, coffee on the desk. Now that is where I want to start, how about you and Kron?" asked ClairOn.

"Sed and Kron, I can tell you that our staff on our other terraformed planet, Gametes, have been moved off planet on two of our battleships. We left the center with an appearance of liveliness to give a targeted appearance of an active base," said Clairon with a large smile.

Sed turned and looked at his husband, Kron, and asked, "what do you think of all this Kron?"

Kron replied, "Sed, I think we have no choice but to stoke the fires of this hell we have been forced into. I pray we aren't forced to use our hidden weapon. One way or another we are forced to find a resolution of this nightmare and that QuaRen. I don't understand what happened to our culture that a murderous and judgmental belief would soon dictate to us and force us into this damn civil-war."

"I think our battleships should be enough especially with our deflective shields. So, you two what is this hidden weapon you just mentioned," asked ClairOn.

Sed replied looking straight on to ClairOn, "sorry ClairOn but I won't discuss that now and hopefully never, never will," replied Sed.

The base command deck staff were now quite comfortable at this hidden station after settling in for the past five days. Many missed the glass walls of their former station that gave them a beautiful view of nature as it surrounded that base. Here, while comfortable, only walls were their view with this new location buried under the surface of RaedenOvul's moon, Onvus.

Suddenly, upon those solid gray walls a holographic image began showing of their former view through the glass walls on RaedenOvul. This projection had a three-D depth with the movement of wind and moving leaves, clouds and various life forms which appeared as real as ever.

The room burst into screams of appreciation as Kron stood up waving about at everyone. Kron was an expert in holographic imaging and had created an escape from the cold walls of that command deck. Kron was thinking, wait until they see the dining room at lunch today, why even I feel better without those gray walls. Occasionally I felt like those walls were closing in on me which gave me periods of extreme discomfort.

Another week had passed and the work on the base control deck was very relaxed with the view of nature in the holographic images.

"Sed, a call coming in from Commander LynLouOn, do you want it private or on open communication system?" asked Kron. "Put it open, please," replied Sed.

"Commander LynLouOn here Sed. The bad news is that around 8 a.m. our time, the base on Gometes was destroyed by QuaRen. And the best news is that no one was present on our base. All communications, as you ordered, Sed, were a set up to fool that QuaRen and her Guardians. Thankfully we only lost our base and no lives. The attack originated from BathKohl. Just a moment Sed, I have an emergency communication coming in. Oh No!" exclaimed the Commander. Sed stood up from his desk obviously shook-up.

"Sed, this is damn shocking. Apparently, the Guardians and some of their military ships were hidden in the attack and have landed on our other two terraformed planets, but not on RaedenOvul. I think since they were following their striking torpedo's they were afraid of being attack in this quadrant, so they stayed clear. The Guardians have landed outside our base area on Gametes and appear to have landed on our uninhabited Virgo. From my experience, Sed, I would call this a trap in progress as I believe they are waiting for a response with our ships, hoping to take us out," stated LynLouOn.

"Commander, make sure that our only ships approaching Onvus have our cloaked technology as we must do all that we can to keep ourselves hidden," stated Sed. "I'm already on it Sed," replied the Commander.

C HAPTER 19

"THE BEGINNING OF THE END"

"SironLashval, I'm so glad to see you. Thank you for being available so early in the morning. I am hoping that we have achieved our goal of placing all residents of NorisColren who are registered as presently refusing our Ren into the residential zone of our second defense base," stated the QuaRen to her Guardian Commander.

"Yes QuaRen, we have been able to complete your order. As you ordered all residents of NorisColren who have not joined into the Ren have been moved to our second military base, LeeDock," replied Guardian SironLashval. "SironLashval, have we any information on Sed and his staff? According to your attack force there were no bodies found after the attack on his RaedenOvul post.

Wherever his is hiding we must find Sed and all his people and take every one of them out. I have no doubt that they are a threat to our temple itself. The horror Sed represents could bring a great challenge to the flow of our Ren. Our Ren brings freedom and truth to all, regardless of planet or species. We are all a gift of the Ren. Amen," said the QuaRen.

"Amen my QuaRen, Amen," replied her personal and commanding Guardian while standing at attention to the QuaRen.

"Guardian, Please, stand down. Have we captured any vessels that are in allegiance with Sed?" asked QuaRen.

"We found two supply vessels, but we have no information of where they came from nor their destination. They refused to be boarded when one of our battleships discovered them. Their weaponry was minor, but they began to fire at our ship after refusing to surrender. Our battleship attempted to take out their engines but for some unknown reason both of Sed's ships just disintegrated into debris, not even a full slip of paper survived," said the Guardian.

"This is definitely a state of war between Sed and our Ren of which there is only one victory and that is our Ren. SironLashval, how well is our military set for a continued action against this traitor, this sinner?" asked the QuaRen.

"We are well prepared for any military need as you see fit, my QuaRen," responded Guardian SironLashval.

"First, see to it that our defense system for our BathKohl is more than adequate. Then find out what systems exist that are best for discovering the location of Sed. He must be on one of his ships and I want him found. Should he surrender bring him directly to me here and we will make a public spectacle of him and anyone with him. Keep me informed daily SironLashval. Thank you, you're dismissed," closed the QuaRen.

Guardian SironLashval left in a very respectful march while feeling totally uncomfortable after this meeting with the QuaRen. He reflected on how this entire experience was so strange. He couldn't remember any such event in BathKohl's history and was wondering if they would continue down this road of war. I feel like a lost soul on the highway of life, and I truly don't like this.

As Guardian SironLashval approached the security entry for their military post LeeDock, he didn't like this defense base being turned into a prison system. He stopped at the base Command Center to see the names listed as prisoners.

Looking at the rather long list of names he discovered that many scientists were locked up here, shaking his head he wondered truly for what.

It's a shame I can't trust anyone to talk with about my personal issues with this Ren. I couldn't even trust my wife. Here I am responsible; responsible - what is that, sounds like someone coming in here.

The night shift commander entered the communication room, saluting and smiling at SironLashval saying, "Siron, it is good to see you. Anything I can help you with today?" "Commander, I have been wondering how this isolation might be bringing conversion to these residents. I pray that our terraforming scientists are converting as we just don't have any more in that science here on BathKohl than those imprisoned here on this base. Sed must have kept that final formula phase in stabilizing a new planet to himself. If we lose Sed we won't have that stabilizing formula and may be lifetimes before someone figures out the answer. Besides, if we can't get anywhere in conversion of those here then I believe eventually our QuaRen will order that they be freed into the flow of the Ren. And Commander, you know what that means," stated SironLashval with an intense eye-contact to the commander and a strong salute.

CHAPTER 20

"THE SQUALL OF WAR"

The Warship Alonfen had taken on some damage by torpedoes that were exploded near the ship. One smaller war vessel and two patrol vessels had been lost in an unexpected attack near the two moons of BathKohl. The ships that were lost had no shields which made them easy targets.

"Where did those three torpedoes come from" asked Commander LynLinVonet of her bridge defense staff.

Navigator ZinLong replied, "Commander, it appears that the origin of the torpedoes is just about mid-way between our two moons. There was no ship in that location according to our scans, but one scan did find evidence at that Location of a ship's energy trail. Commander, it appears to have similar technology to our cloaking. I'll put our latest recorded scan up on the viewer, Commander, and it is a war ship that is visible when firing those torpedoes. Apparently, its shields must drop when its weapons go online and when they fire. It must be a planet that is foreign to us that is working with the QuaRen. They are excellent and experienced military strategists, and they stay completely undetected unless they fire their weapons. Their engines leave a constant trace element, so we need to have all our ships looking for engine wakes, constantly.

We don't know how many ships we have lost recently but I do know that we have lost two battleships and it appears that we also have lost six shipping vessels and a few trading ships."

Commander LynLouOn faced Navigator ZinLong, saying, "we must stay cloaked and under no circumstances allow any communication. Let's get back to Sed and discuss our problem with these unidentified warships and our information that those who are not following that QuaRen, and her Ren have been placed into confinement at the LeeDock military post."

Sed was at his station in the control center of their moon base Onvus when the warship Alonfen landed at the base.

"Attention, this is your Commander LynLouOn speaking, "First let's get all damage to this ship repaired and then we will have a break here at the base, which I will announce when I think it is time. My second will be in command while I am consulting with Sed."

Sed got up and meet the Commander at the entry door to the control center and as the two of them walked through the center to the conference room all on duty stood up and saluted them. The Commander had wet eyes as everyone saluted her with such unexpected respect. When she and Sed reached the conference room door, she turned, stood to strict attention, and saluted back to the staff.

"Wow Lyn, that was so amazing," stated Sed to Commander LynLinVonet. "Please, sit down Lyn and let me fill a couple glasses of water for both of us. Here you go Lyn, fresh and iced."

They both sat down for a few quiet restful minutes with Sed soon breaking the silence, "Commander, I got your send right after you landed and thank you. The information is upsetting but I must admit I am not surprised that this QuaRen formed a military relationship with someone. I sure would like to know what she is giving up for this military aid. And the fact that they have similar defense technology to hide their ships is extremely worrying. It is good that we thought ahead on this, and we will continue with no communication off this post to you or anyone, especially that QuaRen. QuaRen's Guardians are prepared to trace any such message so we will continue communications through our deflection system. Even with shields up she can trace a straight-line signal and fire missiles, or whoever is working with her will be cloaked and just waiting for our mistake."

"Sed, we have found that even with their shields up we are able to trace their ships from their energy path. We have also learned from our interactions with these new ships that they must drop their shields before they fire so I have ordered constant search for a signal strength which may be an engine source. I hope we discover some of those ships and take them out Sed," said Commander LynLouOn as she enjoyed sipping her glass of chilled water while expressing a sigh of relief. "Commander, how are our civilian ships doing?"

"Not well Sed, not well at all, here is a written report for you on our losses known to date. The QuaRen apparently will go to any lengths to maintain supremacy and control over our home BathKohl and anyone anywhere. Sed, I believe this is going to get far worse than I have dreamed of," voiced Commander LynVinVonet.

"I believe you and our other military ship officers must develop a plan that will best protect our ships and sadly, take out as many military and shipping vessels under control of this QuaRen as quickly as possible. We need various attack plans that appear to be disordered so her Guardians will see no organized pattern in our attacks. Be sure and remind everyone that only you are our source of communication and no signals to or from this base will be tolerated. If we are going to win this war, then this base must remain absolutely hidden. Only shielded vessels are to approach this base and all shielded ships keep their shields up continually unless I order otherwise," ordered Sed to his Commander LynLouOn.

"Commander, we must continue our security as too who is cleared for any information about this base, understood?" stated Sed while leaning over his desk and saluting his Commander with his glass of cold water.

The Commander stood to attention and saluted Sed in return with her glass, "Yes Sir, Sed. If we are finished then, and with your approval I will allow my crew to take a break here on the base while having my ship fully inspected."

"Sounds good Commander, take leave as you see fit and thank your crew for their service. But first, let's discuss our plans and there will be no record of our conversation for our complete safety. And thank you Commander," stated Sed.

CHAPTER 21

"HIDE AND SEEK"

"Commander, the assigned ships are at their stations," said the Communications Officer on the Command Deck, ZinLong, as the warship "Alonfen" pulled within a group of similar sized asteroids in the large asteroid belt of the BathKohl planetary system.

"How is the security of our positioning Navigator ZinLong," asked Commander LynLouOn as she was observing the view screen of the Command Deck which displayed the surrounding materials of their location in this asteroid belt. "Excellent Commander, excellent. As our lab projected, the metals of these surrounding asteroids where we are parked will maintain a stable, undetected position," replied Navigator ZinLong as she continued to observe her navigation screen for any unexpected and dangerous fluctuations of any asteroid.

Commander LynLouOn sat in her command chair finding herself deeply immersed in the scene on the main Command Deck Screen knowing that directly in the center that little miniature white pearl was their lost home of BathKohl, and she knew she wanted that pearl back, shinning again with love and acceptance.

Commander LynLouOn just could not imagine how one person could create such a hell. So many of our planet's mining and support vessels have been lost to those war ships for that QuaRen. Those losses are just unbelievable. It appears that this QuaRen is ordering the destruction of so many ships just to please herself. Why would you destroy mining ships that sell to anyone regardless of their home planet? And on top of that, destroying the mining facilities with total disregard for all women and children.

The Commander turned her chair towards her Communication Officer, ZinLong, saying, "Officer ZinLong, no matter what the subject may appear to be of any incoming communication you do not respond in any way. And that is an order. It just occurred to me if you can shut-off or block all outgoing communications from our ship I order that to be done as quickly as possible," understood ZinLong?"

"Yes, sir commander. I will put that into place as I know of a way to do exactly as your ordered, Sir. I will inform you as soon as I have it completed, sir." "Thank you ZinLong," replied the Commander.

The crew of the "Alonfen" had never known such quiet which was welcomed and restful.

Two quiet days had passed, and the Commander had just stepped onto the bridge when the on-duty lead Navigator was observing his three screens and was drawn to the center screen, observing two blip abnormalities that just appeared. They both were moving slowly, his first thought was that they were moving towards BathKohl but oddly their trajectory reflects more of a lost ship, unless there on a search. That's it, they're searching for us, thought the Navigator.

"Commander, good timing on entering the bridge," stated Navigator ZinLong, "I believe we have two vessels which you can see on our middle screen that are just possibly two cloaking battle cruisers and from what I can see, I don't think they are ours."

"All right ZinLong, show me what you've got," responded the commander while looking into ZinLong's grey sparkling eyes. The commander thought "if only those eyes had such a beauty for me, oh well, I better drop that thought right now".

"Commander, these two insignificant speckles I have been observing have a very controlled pattern. I think these are two battleships with cloaking technology that are with the QuaRen. One thing they may not understand is that they leave a detectable energy trail and I think that is what we have here. But there is something odd about their location to each other. It just may be a method of triangulating a target that is cloaked. As soon as the cloaked ship fire's they are triangulated and fired upon immediately and I see that as a ninety percent success in targeting and taking out the target," explained ZinLong.

Thank you ZinLong. I agree with your computation on triangulating a target. That is a simple process to target a cloaked ship. I am not sure about your ninety percent in targeting success, but I find that terrifying, absolutely terrifying," replied Commander LynLouOn.

"ZinLong, have you been successful in blocking all communications from our ship?" asked the Commander. "Yes, sir Commander. I have been able to set up a system that is active and will block any type of communication from this ship. That system can be taken off by using a password I have placed into our navigation system. While I know it personally, sir, you can access the password by breathing onto this device. Your' genetic code is hidden in the outer shell and will respond to your breath. Sir, what about our other two ships if we can't communicate to them about these two cloaked battle-cruisers?" replied Navigator ZinLong

"ZinLong, let me tell you that I truly regret some of the decisions I have had to make concerning this ship and the other two. I just hope that the navigators on the Rilaun and the Dulaun have the same observation that you have and what those two ships are apparently up to." While speaking the Commander was looking out the small port window near the navigations center visualizing the worst scenarios possible. She was hoping to herself that her worst fear was just that and not intuition. "ZinLong, my greatest fear is that both our Rilaun and Duluan just might attack those two ships as they have not understood the triangulation trap you computed. If our other battleships take action against those two, then sadly we are not to respond or communicate in any way. Understood Navigator?" she stated loudly in here command voice while she turned to her command chair and sat down.

"Yes sir, Commander," replied Navigator ZinLong.

Commander LynLouOn turned on the ships communication system from the left arm of her command chair and placed the ships communication system into its 'security communication level', then she sat back and took a deep breath, slowly exhaling for a moment of relaxation, if possible. "Attention, attention, this is Commander LynLouOn announcing that I am placing our ship on our "high security level". We just may have two of those cloaked battleships from the QuaRen in our quadrant but not in this asteroid belt, at least yet. I am ordering all entertainment and communications systems off, excluding of course all necessary inner ship communications. Over and out". Disappointing to the commander the command decks large viewing screen went black. The Commander hoped this would work as her only experience of this action was in her past training at the "BathKohl Interplanetary Cadet Center." It makes me so angry to think that our training center is now the "Guardian Training Academy".

ZinLong turned in her chair towards her Commander, saying, "Commander, I think you should come over to my Navigation screens as I've got to show you something I don't like". "Okay ZinLong, what have you got?" said the Commander as she left her command chair to see what she had on her scopes.

"Commander, the Rilaun and the Duluan are moving out from their assigned locations and are apparently moving towards those two ships," said ZinLong as she had placed her left-hand over her mouth. "Can't we give them a warning of an apparent trap, Commander," asked ZinLong.

"No, I'm sorry ZinLong but we have no choice and must maintain a total lack of communication no matter what happens. I don't want to believe what is happening right now, this scares me to death. I believe you have been right about this, and it is a trap. It is just too easy. I want to be wrong, totally wrong," voiced the Commander while watching an unfolding nightmare on those three screens as a few tears began showing up in her eyes. "I wish we could warn them about this as you see it, but damn it, we just can't".

Okay everyone, no one leaves the bridge without my approval, nor are you to talk to anyone off the bridge until further notice. I'm placing my bridge on a level two communications blackout. I don't want to know the answer but we're going to see it soon, I'm afraid," stated the Commander.

The crew was watching the navigator's screens as the Rilaun and Duluan approached the two vessels they could locate through their engine exhausts, when suddenly another vessel became visible on screen behind the Rilaun and Duluan, firing their weapons in heavy repetition. The Rilaun and Duluan lost their engines on the first weapons barrage and a second weapons firing destroyed the Rilaun and Duluan with no possibility of survivors.

Verbal anguish took the bridge when the ships were destroyed, followed by silence as everyone returned to their stations.

"I'm very sorry. Our security remains as I ordered. Please remain at your stations. ZinLong, how are we doing on your scopes?" asked the Commander as she looked about her staff.

"Commander, I have another ship approaching and with our location. They are a battleship with shields up, sir," said ZinLong as he looked over his shoulder to the Commander. "Keep our ship exactly as she is with everything off excluding your navigation equipment ZinLong. Could you recognize anything about that ship, and do you think it might just be in the area and not really aware of us?" asked the Commander.

"From that short time, I've been able to see it I thought it might be Sed's ship from our hidden base. But until we could prove that beyond any doubt, I will keep our security as you have ordered, sir," said Navigator ZinLong as she kept an intense watch on her three scopes.

"Commander, that ship has halted in a bevy of large asteroids. I have traced them from energy movement, which is intermittent like our ship, sir. Sir, this may be Sed's battlecruiser. We could transfer a signal that would bounce enough as to hide our location and hopefully get a return that will verify one way or another, if it is Sed, sir.

But, if it is Sed then something must have gone horribly wrong on our hidden base, sir," said ZinLong.

"ZinLong, you wouldn't be our Commanding Navigator if you weren't the best. Send a signal and bounce it in the best way possible that keeps us safe. I will be at my station and hoping it is Sed but wondering why he would be here, unless, no, I don't want to even think that," stated Commander LynLouOn.

A good hour had passed when a return message came in from a separate bounce that ZinLong had used for sending the Commanders communication.

"A message has arrived Commander and it will take your security clearance to open it, Sir," said Navigator ZinLong.

"Okay, I will take it in my office. Please transfer that to my office system ZinLong, and thank you," replied the Commander as she rose from her command station as she 'sighed', turning to those few steps into her bridge office.

Closing her office door, she sat down at her desk and placed her hand on the security reader on the right-hand corner of the front edge of her desk.

The message was decoded while Commander LynLouOn remained standing crossing her arms in disgust of the recent events, "and now this, what next" she thought to herself. Good, she thought, it looks ready to play any second.

"Commander LynLouOn, this is Sed, and I am here with my staff on this battlecruiser that has been pinged. I purposely put out an energy path once I got into the asteroid belt as it is the only safe place to locate you, a risk I had to take. Give me a message in some form that will locate your cruiser. If it works for you, I can first come over to your ship in a shuttle. My shuttle craft has small rocks placed all over it so in slow motion my shuttle should look exactly like a rock. My navigator will keep alert for your response. Thank you, Commander. Sed, over and out!"

Commander LynLouOn thought to herself, "wow, what's next.

First, I lost my other two battlecruisers and now here is Sed out of nowhere, totally unexpected. Something had to have gone horribly wrong at our hidden moon base to have Sed and his staff here in the asteroid belt".

Sed reflected to himself "that if I make it over to the Alonfen in my asteroid shuttle then I must consider my final defense choice. This is undoubtedly the most insane life experience I have had. As Sed was piloting through the rocks, his daydreaming almost caught him head-on with one large drifting asteroid. Sed became more alert as he piloted himself between tumbling rocks of the asteroid belt, squinting every time he bumped harmlessly into a small rock.

"Commander, Sed's shuttle has just arrived and has settled in the Landing Bay. He is being brought up to bridge right now."

With that message the Commander got a couple mugs of coffee ready, knowing that Sed loved a fresh mug of coffee no matter what. The elevator door opened and Sed entered the command deck heading right over to the Commander, "Sed, welcome and here is a mug of good ole coffee for you. So, what has happened Sed?" asked the Commander as she saluted Sed with her mug of coffee.

"We discovered a cloaked enemy battlecruiser in line with our moon, so I ordered everyone to board our battlecruiser and we left with shields up and good thing I ordered it as within five minutes our base was destroyed. So here we are now Commander. How are your three ships doing Commander," asked Sed.

"I'm sorry to tell you this Sed but we have lost both the Rilaun and the Duluan just a few hours ago. They were destroyed and all hands lost by an attack from three battleships under the command of QuaRen. And now we have lost our moon base. How did that happen Sed?"

Sed's answer was, "that apparently we had a traitor amongst us all this time. A lady in our science lab was discovered to be a believer in this RenCeti. Our freshman navigator, Kor, discovered the hidden communication and notified me immediately and I immediately ordered total evacuation and brought the traitorous lab technician with us. After we arrived here in the asteroid-belt I had that traitor ejected out of a torpedo shaft.

And now unfortunately I believe we have no choice, and with your required assistance, to activate my final weapon. Unless Commander, you have an alternative, my final weapon must be activated."

"There is no other answer Sed, none. What would you have us do?" asked the Commander. There was silence on the bridge as the staff listened to the conversation.

"Everyone, return to the attention of your stations, immediately," ordered the Commander as she became aware of the silence and the eyes upon her and Sed.

"Commander, I want a message sent to the QuaRen that demands her immediate surrender, giving her 5 minutes to respond and give the message source the illusion of being near BathKohl's Sun. I will allow three minutes after we know for sure that our message was received for her response. In that message I want all her war ships unmanned in one hour after her surrender and in that same hour the battleships that are working for her must take down their shields and exit our quadrant immediately. Also, her Guardians are to be disbanded and disarmed immediately, as well as her active military force on BathKohl.

The QuaRen must remain in her residence until my arrival. Immediately we will discuss my choice in punishment with her. And I want you present in that discussion Commander, you need to keep me from touching her.

And now commander, I'm going to lay down in the guest quarters where I will sleep until you have something for me on this communication with the QuaRen. Okay commander?" asked Sed.

"No problem, Sed. I see your stooping and your eyes and face are showing exhaustion, so I think your choice to the guest room is good and you really need to go now. Sed, I will keep your location quiet and that is so ordered to everyone on duty on my bridge," stated the Commander. "Yes sir" replied the bridge staff to their Commander.

"Sed, as soon as I have a reply from the QuaRen I will come to your quarters so we can discuss our choices," said the Commander as Sed was turning to leave the bridge. Sed stopped for a moment and shook hands with the Commander, turned and headed to the elevator door.

Communications Officer ZinLong was at her Bridge Station developing a method to communicate untraceable to the QuaRen which wasn't as difficult as she thought. ZinLong solved it quickly so any attempt to trace their origin would result in total confusion.

The Commander was slowly waking up as she returned to the Bridge Station (the command deck) and walked over to ZinLong's Navigation Station as she appreciated how attractive ZinLong was to her. ZinLong had a winning swimmer's body, maybe when this is all over ZinLong would go out with me on a date.

The Commander, after a few minutes listening to ZinLong, left the Bridge to go and wake up Sed, "Sed, I am sorry to wake you up right now, but ZinLong has worked out a plan for your communication to QuaRen and she is ready for you on the Bridge."

Sed slowly sat up and turned around to face the Commander, then leaning back against the wall, he said, "Lyn, I had no idea how stressed out I was and how tired I was, but I feel a little more alive now. I wrote out my plan for ZinLong and due to the time as ZinLong perceives it through her plan, she will make the decision as to the moment that QuaRen's time for response has expired. If she doesn't meet the time limit, then I think it best that you and I go into your office and enter our codes to activate our hidden weapon system. Let's go Lyn."

"Yes Sir, Sed. I will follow through with our agreement and complete my side of the code," replied the Commander as they exited Sed's quarters.

"Thank you, Lyn. I'm very sorry that we have arrived at this point, but I see no other responsible choice," replied Sed as they entered the elevator for the Command Deck.

"I'm sorry also Sed, but your' right," replied the Commander.

As the Commander and Sed reached Communication Commander ZinLong's desk, it was no surprise to see three filled mugs of coffee set up, a norm for these three.

"I don't believe I could have designed a better plan ZinLong, great work, thank you. The papers I just handed you, ZinLong, outline my message, and I have extended the return answer time to five minutes, from QuaRen. I'll sit down here and let your carry on ZinLong. What a time this is," stated Sed, as he and the Commander sat down near ZinLong's station.

ZinLong inputted the communication, hit her send, and sat back telling Sed and the Commander that the message had been sent and her pre-set timer was in progress. The bridge was very quiet since Sed entered the bridge.

Sed thought quietly to himself how much he wanted to return to BathKohl, to have the peace they had always known before this QuaRen, to return to their spiritual life.

Commander LynLouOn had returned to her station on the bridge after walking around to all the stations, leaving a beautiful filled wine glass at each station, saying, "I have poured a great wine for everyone and now would like everyone to take your glass and when I say this man's name at ZinLong's station, let us all salute him for his endless work for peace and to return our BathKohl to its historical heritage of acceptance, love, and respect for all. Salute!

After a salute to Sed everyone placed their glass down and gave Sed a resounding applause, bringing Sed to a few cheers himself as he looked around the bridge, returning the salute with his glass.

After everyone returned to their duty stations Sed sat down to wait in silence, waiting for the return message, hoping that surrender would be the reply.

After thirty minutes had passed, Sed rose from his chair and in a slightly emotional moment, chokingly he said, "I'm so sorry ladies and gentlemen but it does appear that QuaRen still believes she and her RenCeti are yet the only true path. To herself she is right about her reasoning for the many outright murders on BathKohl, committed in the name of her RenCeti.

And now, if our Commander agrees, I think it is time for a staff change on the bridge so all of you can take a break." The Commander stood up and said, "I'm following Sed's advice everyone and we will change shifts now. Enjoy your dinning and get a good night's sleep."

Sed went with commander LynLouOn to dine in her quarters where Sed began an important conversation," from what you said Commander we have lost our other two battlecruisers with numerous other ships. We have arrived at a point of no other choice but to warn this QuaRen that if she and her Guardians continue on their present path and do not immediately surrender in their return message, again, five minutes after receiving our demand for surrender. If I do not receive that surrender, then I will order the activation of my hidden weapon which will end this nightmare of disgrace and death by our history's only murderer, the QuaRen. In that message, I order that the QuaRen, her supporting staff, and her Guardians must all be in the Public Arena at the LeeDock Military Base at my ordered date and time and must be completely disarmed. There, residents will be inspected for hidden possession of any weapons as I list them. Here, let me give you this Commander, an exact written copy of what I want communicated to this QuaRen. I only want your Communications Officer ZinLong to see this and communicate this. Perhaps we can wait in your bridge office for her response?" stated Sed.

"No problem, Sed. ZinLong and my Bridge Staff will be on duty through this, Sed," stated Commander LynLouOn.

The Commander and Sed entered the Bridge while the Commander's full staff was present and attentive at their workstations. Sed handed ZinLong his handwritten communication, then Sed gave the order for transmission, then Commander LynLouOn and Sed went into the Commanders Bridge Office.

The entire staff continued to work in silence as a chill spread through Bridge.

As the Commander and Sed walked through the door, Sed stated, "I expect an answer within the hour, one way or another and I just hate this. So now we're into a countdown mode. I just hope QuaRen understands that I am telling her the truth and she has no choice but to accept my demand. But, truthfully Lyn, I don't believe she will accept my demand."

CHAPTER 22

"BREAKING POINT"

QuaRen was in her office at RenCeti's Temple when the message came in from Sed presenting the surrender terms. QuaRen was frozen in her chair with the greatest anger she had ever known. She continued to stare at her screen monitor in total shock and disbelief as she read Sed's message a number of times.

"Siron, come over here and look at this message from Sed.

Do you believe this, a life threat from Sed to all of us? Isn't there any way Siron, that we can trace this message in our response to Sed so we can take out this sinner and his followers?" asked QuaRen.

"I'm sorry QuaRen but from our previous attempts to trace where Sed is at from his messages have all failed. Even with our embedded tracing codes we have no information," replied SironLashval, Commander of the QuaRen Guardians.

QuaRen paced behind her desk for a few minutes and then turning to Siron, said, "that from Sed's communication we have only a few minutes to respond and he say's if we want peace our entire RenTahn, your QuaRen, and our Guardians must all surrender. We cannot capitulate to someone full of such evil that he would end our RenTahn. My message in return to him is that he is the one who must surrender and surrender to myself. Siron, inform him that I have ordered all citizens of NorisColren who have not joined our RenCeti in one hour from this message's delivery are to be freed from their sins for the good of each soul and for the good of RenTahn. I've changed my mind Siron, just send the answer in one simple word, no. Place our entire defense on emergency alert as we have no idea what this Sed might attempt so we must be prepared." following this statement the QuaRen left her office and went into the Temple.

C H A P T E R 23

"WINNING IS NOT ALWAYS VICTORY"

Sed and Commander LynLouOn were sitting at Communications Officer ZinLong's communications station when QuaRen's reply to Sed's demands arrived.

"Okay ZinLong, go ahead and read her reply and it is okay to speak strong enough for the entire deck staff to hear," stated Sed.

"Attention everyone. I have been given permission to share this response to Sed's communication that the QuaRen must surrender, and it is short, in capital letters, 'NO'. There are no other words," announced ZinLong.

"Oh, I have received a second response. Shall I read it to all Sed?" asked ZinLong of Sed.

From the QuaRen, "There will be no surrender by your QuaRen or my Guardians. I have ordered the freeing of all those of NorisColren who have not joined us in the RenCeti, by my command, that is underway at this moment. There will be no future communications with you Sed so don't waste my time," read ZinLong.

The Commander and Sed stood up and slowly turned observing the response of their present staff, reading their faces, a mix of shock and sadness.

"Ladies and gentlemen, I am so sorry for what we have just heard, and I believe it is already too late to stop what this QuaRen has ordered of her Guardians," said the Commander strongly to all as everyone shed tears.

After a few minutes of silence, both the Commander and Sed saluted the Command Deck and exited to the elevator, going to the Commanders quarters and entered quietly, both sitting down.

The Commander went to her cooler and took out a bottle of her favorite wine, opened it and poured that wine into two beautiful crystal wine glasses, handing one to Sed as she remained standing, looking at Sed.

"Sed, this is truly an anguish that I just don't understand but I want to give a salute to those we may be losing today and to those who have stood up against this QuaRen no matter what the cost. They both saluted and then drank their wine.

"Commander, do you have any idea on how we have done with our inoculation against my weapon," asked Sed "Unfortunately, I have no numbers, but I do know that we have a large success due to our underground movement, and substantially within the Guardians. I think we will see a very large number of survivors, especially due to the large amount of serum production we had to do to keep up with the demand. I believe most, if not all members of our Terraforming Crew have been inoculated, along with most of our interplanetary miners and traders. There is an unknown count of those who refused the shot as no Doctor would answer their inquiries as to what this inoculation was for," replied the Commander to Sed while sitting on the edge of her office desk.

"I'm so glad to hear about high demand and production. Unfortunately, Commander, we have been pushed into an impossible corner and our only way out is to move forward. I see you have my matching key on your desk Lyn. First, let's have another glass of wine in honor and memory of those we have lost and that we will soon loose. Salute Lyn, salute. Now, let's take our keys to your bridge and key our response to this QuaRen. I must act now Commander, or I may not if I delay," stated Sed while holding up his glass of wine in another salute.

As Sed and the Commander entered the bridge, the Commander said, "Officers of the Deck, I have placed this bridge at this time on 'red alert' so please remain active at your posts. Sed and I have a command to activate here on the bridge in response to the QuaRen and her Guardians and her RenCeti members that have refused to surrender."

Sed and the Commander both lifted off a neck-chain with a square card on each as they walked over to the Commanders station chair, placing each card on the reader located on each chair arm, then placing a finger on that card after it was placed on the reader.

Then Sed, noticing all watching their action, looked around at the crew, stated, "May I please have your attention, thank you. As you all probably know, I have just set into action our weapon of final choice. As I said earlier, we will get out of this corner, but I don't see it as a welcomed victory, but it will be a victory. We have lost so many ships and they're crews that without this choice we would have lost our BathKohl, each other, and our heritage of a peaceful, loving spirit."

The bridge became quiet as it were completely empty of personnel.

Commander LynLouOn's battleship remained in hiding where they both had been parked for some days in the asteroid belt, a definite stealth location from the QuaRen.

In 72 hours, Sed realized that their home of BathKohl, their terraformed planets, and all trading would be changed forever, all within seventy-two hours of triggering this final defense weapon. Once that action had been set in motion there was no choice to alter that decision.

Four days later, after the activation of Sed's final weapon, the two battleships left their hiding place in the asteroid belt and returned to BathKhol, both ships landing at their Capitol City of NorisColren (Talking Center).

As crews left their ships, each was in uniform and armed. No one had ever experienced the stench that filled the air as they left the ships. As they marched to their city center, there were bodies all over the area. They entered their Capitol office building which the QuaRen had renamed, "RenTahn", the physical center of QuaRen's religion, "RenCeti".

When Sed and the Commanders crew approached this former temple of RenTahn, they were shocked to see the QuaRen was alive. She was standing at the top of the steps.

Since she couldn't have received an inoculation, much to everyone's shock, the QuaRen could have only survived if she was a lesbian.

Everyone walked up the steps towards the QuaRen in total disbelief.

Sed immediately spoke to the QuaRen, "QuaRen, I am astounded that I see you standing here alive," as the Commander stood to right of Sed and the other crew members on various steps below them.

"Sed, this is not your NorisColren but truly it is the Temple of RenTahn, it is the home of RenCeti that is the water of our spiritual flow which you have turned into a desert, a desert of the lost. How could you do this Sed?

Why?" asked the QuaRen as she looked upon Sed and all she could see on the steps.

Sed stood at a rigid attention with his eye's strongly locked on the QuaRen, saying, "QuaRen, you are now under arrest, and you will be housed from this moment forward at our military base, LeeDock, indefinitely. My Commander LynLouOn will assign four men, fully armed, to transport you to LeeDock and lock you up in isolation.

QuaRen, you are the most despicable person I have ever known and the only murderer, guilty of ordering uncounted murders in the name of your sick, sick belief.

Murdering people is your greatest thrill, truly for you a joy! All right, guards, get her out of here. Your belief, a true hell in our history. Commander, get this person into isolation, and I mean total isolation at LeeDock."

As the QuaRen was surrounded by four armed men, she held out her right arm, pointing at Sed and stating in a high, angry voice, "And you Sed, your weapon has murdered more than you seem to be concerned about." The QuaRen was led out of the area to LeeDock.

Sed ordered the QuaRen to stop as he pointed at her and said loudly, "Your followers would have continued this murdering binge of yours, here on BathKohl and eventually on other planets if the future would have allowed it. If your' so right about your RenCeti than why did you join with another military group to take us out. You destroyed numerous ships with destruction of each ship and their entire crews, why? You're the ultimate evil person that I have ever known. You left me with no choice but to use my final weapon, you QuaRen, you! You are to blame for this nightmare, it is all upon your shoulders. Winning is not necessarily a victory, but you left us with no choice!

Commander, get his creature away from here and into isolation where she can meditate the rest of her born days on what she has done."

C H A P T E R 2 4

"Home, the Origin of Unity through Separation"

*T*he first three months following the end of this war many who were deceased from the action of the QuaRen and from the "Weapon of Finality", were buried and memorialized in the many spiritual pathways of BathKohl.

Sed had shared with his Commander that it had been a harsh and tragic victory. And that he was thankful to his Commander for her aid in his preparation of a broadcast to be sent to everyone on and off planet. It was open to anyone, anywhere, to observe.

At the beginning of their fourth month their return to BathKohl, a meeting was set at Capital Building of Bathkohl, "NorisColren" which was set to be a live broadcast to everyone, on and off planet.

Sed began his broadcast stating, "I thank you everyone for your time today and allowing me to share the following information. I have been asked to give a short history of the weapon that ended this damned war.

First, my weapon was developed out of an error that showed up in our initial terraforming research. In stage two, where we were, life had been forming on our first terraformed planet. My team and I noticed something very strange in this period in that there was an unusually high death rate in many of the life forms. Our investigation started within twelve hours of this problem, and we discovered an unintended genetic accident. We discovered in our lab work that this genetic error was stable and suddenly I realized it could be used as a weapon. While this scared me, it didn't stop me from developing it as a weapon. There are two others from my lab staff who have knowledge of this gene structure, and how it works. I shared this with Commander LynLouOn as it became the final weapon for potential use in the rising revolution against the QuaRen and her growing control and her suppression of any belief outside of hers.

What happens in the functioning of this weapon is a gene structure that wraps around the already existing heterosexual gene structure and the bi-sexual coding that is dominantly heterosexual. There begins immediately a destruction of the heterosexual gene structure and causes death within seventy-two hours. After seventy-two hours this gene structure decays and becomes useless. At present we do not know who the QuaRen contracted to aid in her military goals. I expect to discover who they are as we are now going through all QuaRen's files and those of her Guardians.

Now, I will move on with the information I believe most of you are really waiting to hear.

As you know, for the last two months, our BathKohl governing body along with a number of assigned subcommittees were formed to listen to, discuss, and develop your goals in our healing process. While I admit I was very surprised at your goals, you all have my total support. And my terraforming crew told me they are also in total support of your goals. These planned separations are not a show of division but truly a gift to each other of our unity.

By everyone's participation and with one-hundred percent support we will expand to three planets. By mutual decision, our "community of men"[18] will reside on our home planet, BathKohl.

---

[18] "Community of Men: - Gay (men)

By request and agreement our first terraformed planet, RaedenOvul, will become the home to our "sisters and brothers of union"[19].

And finally, in our discussion by request our second terraformed planet, Gametes, will be the home of our "Sisters"[20], announced Sed.

Suddenly everyone in the meeting hall filled the air with spontaneous joy as they jumped in front of their seats, shouting, "thank you Sed, thank you".

As everyone left the capitol meeting hall of NorisColren they were holding hands and moving almost in a dance step of exuberance.

Sed and Commander LynLouOn remained seated in the presentation floor as everyone was leaving and the Commander turned to Sed, saying, "this is just truly amazing Sed where such love has returned. We have returned, in a sense, to our normal Sed. I see that life unravels in a beautiful way when we don't work at it. Your terraforming work has become such a blessing to us all. What appears to be some type of separation is an amazing unity in truth, a definite reward out of our past where freedom, respect, and humility had been our foundation on BathKohl.

In only a few years after Seds announcement, the citizens of BathKohl had completed their work in preparation to colonize Sed's terraformed planets.

During those years a dedicated science team developed a system for "the Community of Men" on BathKohl to create their own babies. One set of male sperm could be turned into an egg and then be fertilized and generally incubated in an artificial womb. The other choice that some did accept was to have a womb implanted in a male body. The "Sisters" also adopted this process to conceive their own children.

---

[19] "Sisters and Brothers of Union: - Heterosexual

[20] "Sisters" - Lesbian

Within four years the agreed goals of BathKohl were completed and the two terraformed planets finally colonized.

The three planets joined together, formed a Planetary Union which was named after their home planet, BathKohl, "the Planetary Union of BathKohl".

Chapter 25

"David dates Maurehn"

"Sed, this is the most astounding story I have ever heard. I'm feeling so excited from your history that I don't feel tired, but I bet you that if I slipped into bed I would fall right to sleep, like a rock. If I hadn't heard this story from you, Sed, I would never have believed a word of it. Amazing, I think It is near noon so that means we did this for a good full day, simply amazing," said David.

"Your' right David, I started telling you this story around noon yesterday. I think David that we best get some sleep now, returning here tomorrow at noon, but I can't decide whether to eat something or just crawl into bed. See you here on your favorite veranda tomorrow for lunch and my planets favorite drink, coffee."

David was not disturbed for his missing his morning physical therapy class and smiled as he woke-up at Eleven a.m., stretching and feeling so good after such a long sleep. A nice shower and fresh set of clothes and he was ready to meet Sed again, he might be a little late, but he thought Sed probably would be l late also.

As David walked onto the veranda, Sed was sitting in his usual chair and lunch had arrived. David thought, "Oh boy, their great coffee is ready, and I am ready also".

"Sed, you beat me here. I thought you might be a little late yourself," said David as he sat down for a good lunch.

"Sed, I am amazed that your Great-Grandfather was such a hero in winning that war. And how your society decided to use not only BathKohl, but two of your terraformed planets. You said that your people consider a greater union is formed by your choice to inhabit a planet by one's gender. How is that Sed?" asked David as the two of them were enjoying a very large lunch.

"Well David, I would say that in our spiritual history, excluding that time of that QuaRen and her RenCeti, no national decision ever divided us, rather always created greater unity," replied Sed.

"David, anyone can live on any planet that they want to but most of us like living within our sexual cultures. My Great Grandfather hated that war, and he absolutely hated the weapon he developed. He told me that it was discovered in a terraforming accident from which he refined the results due to a meditative experience he had. After that weapon was mass produced in a totally secured structure with the aid of some of his terraforming staff and then placed in satellites around all our four planets. Only my grandfather Sed could activate this weapon but by his choice it did require one other person to complete the same action at the same time and with her acceptance, that was Commander LynLouOn. This weapon structure enters the body and once recognizing the gene structure of a heterosexual, it brings immediate decay to the brain, heart, and lungs, ending in death within forty-eight hours.

Sed's staff developed a countermeasure which you would call a vaccine. Those inoculated were totally resistant to this weapon.

Now David, I will get on with a few more questions that you wrote down here. Let's see, you asked about how we kept our terraformed planets isolated and safe for their own development from any type of outside foreign contamination.

Before we terraformed, we were building our defenses and constructed five battleships and some small well-armed cruisers. At the same time our battleships were under construction, Kron and his staff were specializing in defense and developed our invisibility cloaking fields which were then placed on our battleships and a few other types of ships. Those cloaking fields could deflect any type of weapon, but a solid weapon, like a torpedo can get through those invisibility cloaks.

We assigned one battlecruiser to each terraformed planet which included their moons for the purpose of keeping them clear of any unwanted foreign ships which could contaminate our work.

One of the biggest known problems were some of the interplanetary traders who are illegal in many actions as they look anywhere to gather something to sell. Our signal throughout our system warned all crafts to stay one-half million miles from any designated location within the communication. We sent out periodic warnings that our terraformed planets and their moons were off limits even to the claim of an emergency and for an emergency one of our vessels would immediately respond.

I see one of your questions is how our planets, and basically, our solar system, are hidden from being displayed on a view-screen.

I did get permission to give you a little more on this. After Kron and his staff developed our ships cloaking system following the closing of our war with the QuaRen, he and his staff were having a lunch break in their lab when suddenly our defense warning system went to Red, and everyone ran to the Defense Room.

The Defense Staff pointed out that on their view-screen five separate flickering lights were visible and the tracking information matched the ships that had aided the QuaRen. The foreign battleships were all ordered to leave this quadrant and never return as they would be fired upon immediately.

Two out of five of those ships came close to BathKohl and launched torpedoes towards our capitol city of NorisColren.

The torpedoes were intercepted and immediately those two ships were hit by return fire and destroyed with no survivors.

Following the energy paths of the three destroyed battleships that attacked our capitol city to their origin led us to meeting a new race, the Klingon's. A communication was sent in numerous repetitions to the Klingons which stated that under no situation were any of their ships to enter our quadrants and the mapping of our quadrant borders were included in those communications.

So, out of that confrontation came a great idea with superb results from Kron and his research staff. They found a new method to power the cloaking shield to such a point that our entire planetary system could be surrounded by this cloak. It is more advanced than our ships cloaking because it will send to a viewing screen a display stars, massive empty space, and even a very dangerous black hole. This has created in our system the best security we have ever known.

Presently our trading system is structured to lead others to believe that our traders are an independent group living on ships with no home planet. Many offered our traders a place to live but as we kept turning them down, they finally dropped their offers.

This is an excellent story line that has made our hidden home planetary system more secure.

I never dreamed we would colonize our planets and it may be that without this war with that QuaRen it wouldn't have come around so quickly.

I have permission to tell you David, that although we have hidden from all other civilizations for many, many years, our experience with you David brought about discussion on opening an ambassadorial relationship with your Federation. As I understand, the present majority is leaning to establishing a meeting with your Federation.

David, I have a great surprise for you. I have finally received clearance for you to spend some time with my terraforming crew. You will have your own private residence near our terraforming main lab."

David replied a little loudly, "Yes, yes, thank you Sed, thank you! I don't know what else I could say but thank you!"

"David, I think you have said it."

While Sed and David were talking, Kron had walked onto the veranda and stood listening to them near the food cart.

"Welcome Kron," stated Sed as he rose up from his chair, greeting his husband with a hug and a kiss. Holding hands with Kron, Sed turned towards David saying, "David, let me introduce you to my husband Kron. Kron this is David that you have heard so much about."

"David got up and looking at them both, saying, "I'm very happy to meet you Kron. I am amazed almost beyond belief that I get to join your terraforming lab. This is just so great. Thank you Kron."

Kron replied to David while enjoying the city view, "If it's not a problem David, you can come along with me right now and I will introduce you to my lab and my staff, after that I will show you to your new residence. I'll see you later Sed, love you."

Kron led David down a long hall which on their right side was glass-wall, which overlooked their beautiful Capitol city. They soon came to a metro like transport car and boarded it.

"In a couple of minutes David, we will be at my main Lab. I doubt you have ever seen our transport system" said Kron as he and David boarded the transport.

"That's true Kron. It is so quiet and so comfortable. I feel no vibrations which is amazing."

The car came to a comfortable stop and Kron led David out into the hallway which appeared spotless.

"Here it is David, my main terraforming lab which we call "Grampa Seds" after Sed's great-grandfather who opened the door to our science of terraforming."

"This is some day in my life, Kron. This entry to your lab reminds me of the lab on the ship I was on, "the Baikonur", said David to Kron as they entered the lab.

"Sed did tell me your story David and I find it amazing. I am sorry David for the loss of your ship and crew, but we are all honored to have meet you as our very first representative of your planet Earth and your interplanetary Federation. Now, let me introduce you to my terraforming crew," said Kron as he escorted David around the lab.

Everyone got up from their station and shaking hands with both Kron and David, and many giving welcoming hugs to both. David was totally shocked that he was now a member of Kron's staff and was so welcomed by everyone.

David looked around at the staff after being introduced to each member, he was a little shook-up to see a mix of men and women which brought him to a question, "Kron, I never expected to see any women since you have divided by gender preference on your planets, so how is this?"

"Well David, having separate planets in our choice of gender separation does not divide us on any of our goals and no matter what, we are united-as-one Spiritual Family. And one is free to live on any of our three planets, regardless of one's gift of sexual identity. All careers are open anywhere to anyone such as becoming part of terraforming after some years of successful study.

Everything we do here in our BathKohl system is open to all on any planet. I understand you are a terraforming scientist yourself, right David?" asked Kron.

"David, Sed and I had some serious conversations as he gave me your request to be introduced to our terraforming lab. I had to discuss this with my team first, and now here you are David, a member of our staff. As for any questions you might have of us and our work David, you may have questions which will require security clearance while other questions may be easily answered.

David was introduced to a young lady sitting at her station in the lab while he also observed glass wall that separated the lab from an obviously sterile lab, "David, this is AhbendRaMaurehn, Maurehn, this is David from our medical recovery unit, the very fella who Sed has been talking to you about of the planet Earth," said Kron while he couldn't help but notice that Maurehn's eye's had brightened as she looked at David, they were definitely locked in a very seductive look with each other, and then the two joined into a long, affectionate hug.

"Well, well Maurehn, it looks to me like you and David have something more than a simple welcome here. I think you two will work together very well," Kron said to David with a smile as he gently grabbed David's left shoulder and began introducing him around the lab to the rest of his staff.

"David, AhbendRaMaurehn is my number two here and I'm going to place her as your lead. You'll even get to share her station. She has been prepped as to her responsibility with you David and all basic sharing in our terraforming has been approved. Now, let me take you over to Maurehn's station and she can set you up. I will be gone for a few hours as I'm going to spend some time with my Sed. See you later David," Kron said joyfully as he exited the lab.

Maurehn turned to David as he approached her station, saying, "David, just call me Maurehn. AhbendRa is my degree title in terraforming."

"Thanks, Maurehn," replied David, as their eyes were meeting again in a very sensual expression, and slowly clasped hands while David turned to look through the glass wall, which opened up their first discussion of terraforming.

In David's first two weeks with Kron's terraforming crew he had been residing in his hospital room and completed a few scheduled medical exams. At the end of those two weeks David was informed that the medical staff decided he was ready to be transferred to the terraforming lab's residential wing.

The beginning of David's third week he returned to his medical room to gather up his belongings and was surprised to find five complete sets of clothing and three pairs of shoes that had been all laid out on his bed with a note stating, "time for a change of clothes David."

When David moved into his own residence it was just a short walk from the lab. During these first three weeks David grew very close to Maurehn and at the same time developed a great friendship with Kron's terraforming crew.

David began meeting Maurehn at his favorite dinning spot, the alcove at the glass walled view of the city. One evening after dinner at the alcove, he and Maurehn held each other in a steady gaze, slowly bringing their faces together and sharing their first kiss, long and sensual. As they returned to their chairs to finish their evening meal, David exhaled slowly and deeply, staying hand in hand with Maurehn for a few minutes.

Eventually, one evening, after their dinner together at the alcove, they slowly walked to David's quarters, closed the door and moved to adventurous love making.

It didn't take the terraforming crew long to figure out that David and Maurehn and drifted into an intimate relationship.

Finally, after many days, Kron and Sed were able to relax together and just sit for some time in their residence, with no calls or knocking at their door.

"Kron, while it's been great to see David and Maurehn fall in love, it is really sad that we are about ready to return David to his people. Unfortunately, they will have to separate from their relationship as

Maurehn will never be allowed to go with him," stated Sed over their dinner table.

"This will be difficult for the two them. But on the other hand, what doors open to us out of this relationship can only benefit all of us. I had a vision about this that I need to share with you, Sed, but I want to keep it for the time being just between us," said Kron. "I have no problem with that Kron," replied Sed.

"I believe David's Earth is a place in our future that will open our first interplanetary direct communications after our war with the QuaRen. Of course, we must bring this up to our council for discussion and a vote and I think the sooner the better. That may be in a few years yet. I see our first ambassadorial relationship will be with Earth and their interplanetary union. I also see us trading ship personnel within the Star Fleet of their Federation. I believe we will join together in space exploration and scientific studies," said Kron.

"So, do you have any ideas on how we might handle this relationship between David and Maurehn," asked Sed of Kron.

"Sed, I think that I will first have a conversation about this problem with Maurehn, and more as her lab commander than a friend. Maurehn cannot return with David, and she will have to change their relationship soon, regardless of how rough that will be. Perhaps it will be easier for her if you tell her of your premonition which I see as reality Kron, but we can't have Maurehn go with David as that future, your premonition Kron, might be changed and that change would not be good. I have no doubt she will accept our need regardless of her intimate loss," said Kron.

The next day in the lab, Maurehn looked over her shoulder at David and said, "David, today you're privileged to enter our sealed lab so follow me. Just follow my instructions David and soon we will be ready for entry. I am sure you now know this is where we work with our most stringent formulas in our terraforming steps. This lab is where we study and further develop our initiating formulas of terraforming. Now follow me into our entry area and please do exactly as I instruct you David."

As David was in the lab-entry he was suddenly dreaming that he was back on Mars, getting ready for that walk on the Mars Curiosity Historical Trail. Then he was aware of the present and being in the entry to the initiating lab. He told Maurehn that he had been daydreaming so would she please start over from the beginning.

Early in the evening David returned alone to his quarters and sat down in his front-room. He was thinking how he would acquire that complete formula before his return to Earth. With his health back to normal he knew it wouldn't be too long before he would be going home.

Kron and Sed headed to the lab after a hearty breakfast with each other, no phone calls and no knocking on their door. Kron stopped Sed outside the main door into the lab and said, "Sed, I am privately concerned about David and our initiating terraforming formulas and methods. My intuition is warning me that David intends to and will acquire much of our initiating process without our permission for him to share with his mother and for that matter, his Federation."

"Sed replied, "I hope you're wrong Kron, so totally wrong on this. But let's keep on our toes for any possible actions that might support your intuition."

When Kron and Sed entered the lab, they were meet by Maurehn with a great big hug which warmed the entire room. The staff behind the glass-wall, dressed in their pressure suits all waved to Sed and Kron and they waved back with wide smiles.

"Thank you Maurehn, and why such a big welcoming hug my fair lady?" asked Sed as he enjoined with both of Maurehn's hands.

"Oh, simply because I love you both," replied Maurehn.

Later that day in the main lab David's former Nurse, RhazLason came in and spent some time in conversation with Kron and Sed. Sed got up and walked to the front door with RhazLason and then went over to Maurehn's desk, asking her, "Maurehn, is David inside our sealed lab with the others?"

Maurehn turned a little surprised and said, "Yes, David is with the crew, and he is learning very well. There is a tremendous similarity between his studies and ours, but the math takes a little work in the transition of styles. So, how can I help you Sed?"

"I tell you what Maurehn, if six this evening isn't an issue, how about you, David, myself, and Kron have dinner together on the veranda with David's favorite view of our Capitol. How does that sound to you Maurehn?" asked Sed.

Maurehn replied, "I think that will work out well as the lab crew should be finished with today's work long before that time. So, we will see you two for dinner this evening."

As Kron and Sed waited on the veranda for their dinner guests, a beautiful sunset sparkled throughout the visible city.

David and Maurehn arrived right on time Sed's dinner invite and were able to see the beautiful sunset. Then everyone filled their dinner plates and sat at the dinner table which already had the water glasses filled.

David asked of Kron and Sed, "Are we having a dinner celebrating for something fellas?" "I'll let Kron handle the good news," replied Sed.

Kron looked at David with a big smile saying, "David, our medical crew said that your recovery has gone excellently and that we can now make arrangements for you to go home."

"Wow, thank you. This is such good news, fantastic. How will you two get this worked out?" asked David as he looked back and forth at Kron and Sed.

"David, this will surely take some work and so we appointed Commander LynLouOn to handle this although Kron and myself, along with many others will work this out. It has already been decided that I will board whatever ship receives you, David. We will also return that Emergency Pod with you. And in the mean- time David you can keep on working in the lab and as we get this figured out, we will keep you up to date as we know more. Right now, I think If nothing else, let's call it a night," stated Sed.

Maurehn told David as they were leaving that she was going to spend the evening alone in her residence as she need some good old quiet time, alone.

David decided to drop by the lab on his way home and do a little more research on their initiating terraforming formula. David wanted that formula in his head before he goes home. He remembered that his mother was having a few issues on stability of the terraforming to a stable and safe planet. When David got to the lab, noticed that he was the only one in the lab. David knew it was the perfect time for what he wanted so he sat down at his desk and began studying the process by Seds' grandfather, RonSed. What David needed was to understand and memorize that formula.

"Bingo," said David allowed, then covering his mouth with his right hand and saying softly, "David, be quiet".

David couldn't believe it, he had found the formula and understood it even in the math form of BathKohl, "amazing, just amazing. I will have no trouble remembering it. I'm out of here and to my quarters and then lights out."

That next evening Kron and Sed had Maurehn over to their residence for dinner and that important conversation. Maurehn said she didn't feel hurt but felt sad knowing she had to separate from David, and she knew that in a very short time she would never see him again. Maurehn returned to her quarters and decided it would be best if she let go of David right now, otherwise she would be hurting herself day after day.

The next day Maurehn was sitting at her lab station when David came into work. "David, I wanted to talk with you before we get to work. First, I'm very happy for you that soon we will get you back home. And the other issue is our relationship, while I have enjoyed our time together David, I just want to be social friends from now on. You haven't done anything wrong David, it's what I need to do for myself."

"Well, I never expected that Maurehn. I even sat back dreaming that you might accompany me home, to Earth. So, why this decision, Maurehn?" asked David with a definite puzzled look.

"David, personally I have enjoyed our time together, very much. But I'm just not feeling any movement in myself towards a committed relationship. Sorry David, but I would rather be honest with you than deceive myself," answered Maurehn.

David replied, "that it will be a rough time for me, Maurehn but I wouldn't want to ruin this friendship.

Maurehn looked appreciatively at David and said, "that the lab work will be a big help, I know it will. So, let's get into our schedule for the day or the rest of the staff will be asking us what's going on," replied Maurehn to David as she handed a copy of the goals for the day.

The next day a call came to the lab for David, and he was asked to have dinner that evening with Sed and Kron in their residence after the end of his workday.

CHAPTER 26

"DAVID RIDES THE ICARUS"

Kron meet David at their door, welcoming him in and showing him to the dining table as Sed was in the process of serving the filled dinner plates.

Sed welcomed David and pointed out his seat and the three sat down to dinner, opening the evening with a good wine. After Sed poured the wine, the three raised their glasses in a salute of 'good luck'.

After the dinner they moved to the front room and sat back in very comfortable chairs, like the old Lazy Boy recliners of Earth's past.

After they sat down in the front-room, Sed stated, "David, we have good news for you from Commander LynLouOn. She was going to be here but wanted to do more research on what she has come up with. She said that she planned on returning to the quadrant where you were found on her battlecruiser when to her navigator's surprise, a vessel from your Star Fleet was discovered and appears to be on a regular patrol in that area with a consistent, repetitive path.

The Commander's navigator is a great historian and loves researching star mapping. In her studies of your Star Fleet, she has recognized this ship as one of your Daedalus class starships. David, you might know this ship from the identification which is "NCC – 178 U.S.S. Icarus". Have you heard of this ship at all David?"

David answered, "Yes, I remember the name "Icarus" somewhere, but I only remember a little about it. I believe the Icarus does quadrant mapping for Star Fleet. Whatever your Commander and her Navigator have put together are facts that are shallow memories right now. Figuring all that I have been through I'm not surprised about having a memory in moments of recollection."

Kron joined in, "David, I believe together we can work out a plan to get you back to your people thru this "Icarus". Sed and I will accompany you onto this Icarus and will make our first introduction to your people. Sed has been given the title and responsibility of our Ambassador to your United Federation of Planets."

David replied, "Are you serious. He is the best choice you could make. Congratulations Sed."

"Thank you, David. My name will stay the same between us but if you remember on how we do titles with our names, then in any formal meeting, such as when we're aboard 'the Icarus', I must be referred to as "ShaNeenSed". Sha is our word that is the same as your word, ambassador. But, as I said, alone between us I am just 'Sed'."

"That I will remember Sed, and I am honored to be introducing you as the Ambassador of 'the Union of BathKohl' too 'the United Federation of Planets'. And now if I might, Kron would you join me in a salute to "ShaNeenSed", stated David as he and Kron stood up, saluting with their glass of wine to Sed and Sed got out of his chair and stood at attention.

"Thank you Kron and David, and I salute you David in great appreciation for your ever-growing friendship, and Kron, for your love," as all three gently touched their wineglasses in an honorable 'chime'.

A few days later a lunch meeting was set up at David's favorite veranda view. When David arrived there, he was welcomed by Commander LynLouOn, Sed, and Kron.

After they all sat down, Commander LynLouOn was looking at David and said, "Welcome David, and as you say, we're just going to pig out and talk. I can share good news with you three as our goal far is being resolved much easier than I originally thought it would be. It occurred to me that all we have to-do is place your 'life pod' on my battlecruiser and then with you three we just move right out close enough to be seen by your 'Icarus'. We will not have any shield up and we will not use our invisibility cloak as our intent is not to let your Star Fleet know of our cloaking technology.

Then we will send a live broadcast signal to their bridge asking for an open communication to their captain. On my bridge for live communication, we must have you Sed, Kron, and you David. With the four of us, and especially you David, standing in the visual communication from the very start, we should do well.

When we board David, we must act formal, so you will address me as Commander LynLouOn and introduce Sed as 'ShaNeenSed', and Kron will be properly called 'AhbendRaKron'," said the Commander.

A few weeks later David, Sed and Kron, were driven to the military base near RenCeti, LeeDock. There they boarded a transport craft and were taken to Commander LynLouOn's battleship, 'the Alonfen'.

Upon their arrival to the receiving deck of 'the Alonfen' they were greeted by Commander LynLouOn BathKohl's usual way, with hugs around. The crew knew Sed and Kron and welcomed David.

"David, I have heard so much about you. I am so happy to finally meet you," greeted Communications Officer ZinLong while shaking hands with David. "Welcome to our Command Bridge David. This is where I will have you standing with our Commander, and you with Sed and Kron when we open communications to the Icarus of Star Fleet. Well, now that I didn't expect. Commander, I have the Icarus on my station screen. Commander, would like this projected to the Main Screen?"

"Yes, Officer ZinLong, please, place that on the Main Screen," said the Commander.

"Lieutenant Antonio, please page for Sed and Kron to come to the bridge immediately," ordered the Commander as she maintained her attention to the main screen.

"Welcome," said the Commander as Sed and Kron entered the Bridge, joining David and the Commander at her station. "I can hardly believe that on our first day there is the Icarus on our screen. I am going to say hello to them right now, so here we go David. I'm turning it over to you ZinLong."

ZinLong kept an eye on the Icarus and opened their first communication to an Earth vessel, "Greetings to the ship "Icarus" from the ship RaedenOvul of the BathKohl Interplanetary Union. We seek greetings and to meet on your vessel. We await your reply. This is Communications officer ZinLong."

After patient waiting, a reply came to the RaedenOvul, "RaedenOvul, this is the Star Fleet ship "Icarus", Captain Johansen responding to your communication. How may we help You?"

"Captain Johansen, this is Captain LynLouOn of the RaedenOvul. I am assigned to open a relationship with you. I see you well on our screen, do you have visual contact from us on your screen?" asked Commander LynLouOn.

"Yes, we have visual contact, thank you," replied Captain Johansen of the Icarus.

"Glad to hear that Captain Johansen. To begin with you will notice I am standing here with three other individuals. On my left is David Marcus, son of Dr. Carol Marcus, of your terraforming science crew. David was formerly a crew member on your Star-fleet vessel, the U.S.S. Baikonur.

And on my right, Captain Johansen, is our Ambassador to your Federation, ShaNeenSed, and to his right is one of our leading Science Officers, Kron, one of our leading science members and husband of ShaNeenSed.

Captain, David Marcus was rescued by a ship from our BathKohl Interplanetary Union and David, after a time of medical recovery, is now ready to return home," said Commander LynLouOn.

"Captain Johansen here. My communications officer is presently checking on David Marcus as I myself have no knowledge of a David Marcus. If you can give me a few minutes to do research on David Marcus, I will be back to you in a short time," said Captain Johansen.

Commander LynLouOn replied, "No problem, Captain, I shall stand by. "After some patient time, communication re-opened between the two ships, "Captain Johansen here of the "Icarus".

"Commander LynLouOn here Commander, open to communication and we will retain our screen broadcast. What might you have Commander?"

"Commander LynLouOn, my communications officer has found that our leader in terraforming, Dr. Carol Marcus, lost her son on our research vessel, the U.S.S. Baikonur in the same area where our vessels are meeting."

"Excuse me, Captain Johansen, I am David Marcus, son of Dr. Carol Marcus. I was a student on the Baikonur when an unknown ship attacked us and destroyed the Baikonur. I survived as I was ordered to enter a life-pod by my Lab Commander which saved me. I was rescued by a sister ship to the one I am on now. When we board 'the Icarus' we can take the time needed to discuss my rescue and my medical recovery by this ships home planet, BathKohl. Now, I will turn this back to Commander LynLouOn," stated David Marcus as he turned to the Commander, nodding his head towards her."

Commander LynLouOn looking at Captain Johansen on the large screen, said, "Captain Johansen, I think it best to work this out aboard your ship. We have a transport vessel that we can use for our transfer, and onboard our transport vessel is the life-pod that saved our friend, David, who we will return to you as I believe it is property of Star Fleet," Captain Johansen was also thinking to herself at this time, "now there is one handsome stud for a commander. I would love some isolated time with him for an exchange of what else but information of great personal importance."

"Commander LynLouOn, you're cleared for our landing bay. The doors will be open, and an energy barrier will be like a wall between space and our atmosphere. You will have a clear view of our landing deck. I will meet you upon you landing and I am required to have an armed escort. All acceptable Commander?" asked Commander Johansen.

"Yes Sir. We're on our way to your Icarus, see you soon Captain," replied Commander LynLouOn.

Commander LynLouOn had no trouble guiding their shuttlecraft, the BrayLing, through the Landing Bay of 'the Icarus', landing very gently. The Commander opened the door, the steps descended, and the Commander walked down to the deck, she was surprised to see a formal welcoming from Captain Johansen of the Icarus and other officers that were standing at attention, with a number of armed personnel standing to both sides.

Introductions were made around and then they were led to the Briefing Room and seated according to Captain Johansen's guidance.

"Thank you, Captain Johansen, for your welcome and this comfortable room to meet in. We appreciate the water, but we do have a love affair for good coffee. David says you have a great coffee, an espresso I believe. We would be very pleased if you have some of that type of coffee available," said the Commander.

"No problem, Commander. I will introduce you to this machine here in this wall. We call this a replicator. I will simply speak into this speaker and say, 'please make seven large espressos', black. Now you will see what appears to be moving light which is a form of energy that will make cups and the espresso and since I ordered no cream or sweetener or any type or amount, it will be black, as we call it, Commander. And there it is. Give me a moment and I will serve it around."

After the Commander had her first sip of the espresso, she said, "David, and Captain, this is just excellent, I love it. If you don't mind, perhaps you can teach one of us, a little later, how to make espresso, but we don't have any such great machine like your replicator."

"I have had the 'survival pod' checked out and it is original to Star Fleet. Presently, our records in Star Fleet have you, David, as deceased with the entire staff of "the Baikonur" as there was no evidence of survival by anyone onboard. I am pleased to say that our scanning genetically identifies you, David, as the real McCoy.

I tell you what, I'll have a server come in immediately, and everyone order what you would like for dinner and then someone can give me a briefing on David's survival and who and what is "BathKohl", said Captain Johansen.

Following the dinner, Commander LynLouOn said to David, who was sitting next to each other, "David, my bet is that tomorrow you will be headed home and a finally have a reunion with your mother. When we get into a little of your history with us, I will, at some point, turn the history over to you David. I may have not told you, but it would be good for you to share that it is not time for Sed to be with your people yet as we must open formal Ambassadorial relations with your Federation through your Federation President. It looks like your Captain is ready to start David."

David gave an excellent outline of his of his study and research time on the Baikonur, and through the end of 'the Baikonur" and how he was rescued by a ship of "the BathKohl Interplanetary Union". David followed with a quick outline of his rescue and his recovery by a medical staff on the planet BathKohl. He kept his agreement to say nothing about his terraforming knowledge and experience with the terraforming staff of BathKohl.

Captain Johansen said, "Thank you, David for outlining this amazing history of your survival and medical recovery. Commander, Sed, and Kron, thank you and all that have aided in David's rescue and recovery, you're all simply amazing to me, and I must say that I feel such love and acceptance from each of you that I must state that you have my love and support. Everyone, if you will excuse me for a few minutes, I have a private communication that I must accept. I'll be back as soon as possible," said Capt. Johansen, as he rose from his chair and exited the room.

Captain Johansen entered his private Quarters and sat down at his 'library computer terminal' and allowed his genetic security code to be authenticated so he could take the incoming call from the "President of the United Federation of Planets".

"Madam President, Captain Johansen of the Icarus here."

"Thank you, Captain Johansen, Madam President here. Let's go live on the screen, Captain."

Madam President and Captain Johansen communicated for some time. Madam President transferred high security information that was recorded by Captain Johansen which was to be transferred to Ambassador ShaNeenSed. The security level would be given to ShaNeenSed and Captain Johansen was to inform ShaNeenSed on how to use this high security information device and speak to no one else about this. The two signed off and Captain Johansen returned to continue the Federations first meeting with members of 'the Bathkohl Planetary Union'.

Captain Johansen arriving back at the meeting and returned to his chair, that speaking to all, saying, "Thank you all for your patience. Excuse me but ShaNeenSed if I might have you enter the side office just behind your seating, I have something I need to share with you. Everyone, we will only be a few minutes and then if you're all up to it, we will have a ship tour for you, so back in a minute," said Captain Johansen as he walked around the dining table and entered the side-office with ShaNeenSed.

Captain Johansen being informal, sat on the corner of his desk and invited Sed to take the chair in-front of the desk, then saying, "ShaNeenSed, what we share in here is between us only and of our highest security level. Is there anyone that you find it appropriate to share this information with, go ahead and tell me when I am finished.

So, I was just had a conversation with the President of our "United Federation of Planets" and she has asked me to hand you this item which is a communication from her for the goal of opening-up this ambassadorial relationship between our Federation and your Union. It has on it for you only, direct communications to our President which she always prefers to be visual, on screen. Madam President will work with you for our mutual goal of eventually bringing you to the Federation as a formal ambassador to our Federation from your BathKohl Planetary Union. Now, is there anyone that is important to be working with you in this process ShaNeenSed?".

ShaNeenSed replied, "Yes Captain Johansen, I would like to add my husband, Kron. We have worked together in developing this forming relationship with your Earth and your Federation. We are both used to living within projects where the communications of those projects are at the highest security level. So, you can inform your Madam President that I have always shared such a secured level of information with my husband as he has with me."

"That will work perfectly ShaNeenSed. That information device through the great work of your Communication Officer ZinLong is compatible with your highest security," said Captain Johansen as they he got up and opened the door returning to the dinner party.

As they toured 'the Icarus', the Commander and both ShaNeenSed and Kron were astounded as they visited the 'Transporter Room', a science of which they had never heard of. Commander LynLouOn was given the experience of transporting to her Command Deck and materializing at ZinLong's station. ZinLong was informed of what was going to take place so that she could alert the rest of the duty staff, so they certainly didn't want to be shocked into a defensive act when the Commander materializes in front of them.

When Commander LynLouOn materialized on the Command Deck of the RaedenOvul Warship, the entire deck staff had been informed and all standing on the Command Deck when quite suddenly their Commander materialized, near ZinLong's station. The Commander said hello to everyone and as quickly as she materialized, she de-materialized off her bridge (when she did her staff expressed utter shock) and she was just as quickly, back on 'the Icarus' transporter platform pad. She stood smiling and amazed at her first experience of being transported, something none of her people had ever heard of.

Captain Johansen gave both ShaNeenSed and Kron an opportunity to be transported round-trip just like there Commander LynLouOn had just done, and they said, "Yes Sir, were ready to go".

ZinLong was notified and soon at the same time, both ShaNeenSed and Kron materialized on the Command Deck of the RaedenOvul. They both said hello and waved to the staff of the RaedenOvul and then as quickly as they materialized, they both de-materialized and were back on 'the Icarus' transporter platform.

"This is the coolest experience we have had in a long time Captain Johansen," said Kron as he looked at ShaNeenSed and Commander LynLouOn.

Next, the tour moved onto the Docking Port Complex to see how the docking port worked while getting a good look at their shuttlecraft. The shuttlecraft of 'the Icarus' was very similar to the Commanders shuttlecraft of 'the RaedenOvul'.

Next, they meet the staff on duty of the Main Bridge and Commander LynLouOn saw many similarities between the main bridge of both crafts which surprised her.

The Commander, Sed and Kron, were delighted to be introduced to each person on duty that evening of the Icarus's main bridge.

Another surprise was the Holodeck of 'the Icarus' which no science on BathKohl had ventured into. The commander, along with Sed and Kron, all really loved the multitude of experiences on the Holodeck. They walked through many areas of the Earth, the Redwoods of Northern California (Kron almost fell on to his back as he looked up to the top of a Redwood Tree and was caught by Sed, the two of them laughed very hard at that moment and the Commander was laughing along with them, covering her mouth as she did. Then they visited the Grand Canyon of Arizona, Death Valley of California, Yellowstone Park, and many other amazing places on Earth and in a very short period-of-time.

It was a long day of introduction to the guests on the "the Icarus", and after the adventures on the Holodeck, they all meet again at the Briefing Room.

Captain Johansen said as they all returned to their seats in the briefing room, "I think we all had a good time with your introduction to my "Icarus" and a number of our ships facilities.

Sed, here is another memory stick with further communication from our Madam President of our United Federation of Planets.

I must say that this day is the most interesting day of my career.

David, I have good news for you. We will be able to unite you with your mother in a couple of days. We will first complete this round of our mapping mission and then we will get you united with your mother."

David broke into the captain's conversation, asking, "Captain, can I call my mother right now and talk to her?"

"No, sorry David, the information given to us stated that we couldn't even talk to her as she is in her secured lab and no outside contact is allowed while she is there. We have talked to her lab security, and they have approved our arrival. Your Mother is very busy, as I was told, working on a problem she is having in her research. She cannot be informed until she exits that lab, and it may be a few days before she leaves that lab. I am not allowed to discuss her research due to the security level of her work," said the captain as he stood in more of a military manner of 'at ease'.

"Captain, if you get permission from Star Fleet, could you take David to re-unite him with his mother in the next few days?" asked Commander LynLouOn of Captain Johansen. "Commander, that is exactly what I want to bring up next. I am cleared to do exactly that for David. What do you think about that David?"

"I am honored Captain and I feel like a nervous wreck about returning not only to my mother, thank you, but to the world I left so long ago. And I 'm also feeling a very sad loss for my many friends on BathKohl.

"David, it's normal having emotional reactions of love and loss. So, Commander, Sed, and Kohl, just let me know when your' ready to return to your ship. And David, you can talk to me anytime about any issue on our mission to get you to your mother's research location," said Captain Johansen.

Within an hour Commander LynLouOn, Sed, and Kron had returned to the Shuttle-deck and were receiving a formal departure with an exchange of salutes.

Then they shook hands and exchanged hugs, giving the longest and strongest hugs to David. As the Commander, Sed, and Kron boarded their shuttlecraft, the three of them were wiping tears as they turned and waved their final good-bye to David, Captain Johansen, and the staff who were standing at attention.

"I had no idea how much I would miss David. This is like losing a son, Commander," Sed stated to the other two as they sat down and prepared for departure.

The three were in a mournful silence as they waited for the Shuttle-craft doors to open which seemed like an eternity to the Commander.

The shuttle-bay doors opened and the BrayLing left for its return to the 'RaedenOvul'.

CHAPTER 27

DR. CAROL MARCUS REJOINED WITH DAVID

"David, welcome to my bridge. We are approaching the system where your mothers' "Federation Research Facility" is located and I thought you would enjoy observing our approach," said Captain Johansen to David on the bridge.

"Thanks Captain. I could see myself recording all that planetary information as we pass through this system as I would have on the Baikonur. Can we see the planet where my mother is at yet?" asked David.

"David, as this is a high security system, this planetary system of your mother's location is only known by my navigator who is the only staff person cleared for knowledge of this system. As you see David, our bridge wall screen is blank, and my navigator is guiding 'the Icarus' to your Mother's Research Facility. Not even I may approach my navigator's station at this time, nor any other staff person navigator is wearing on her uniform which would give you automatic clearance," explained Captain Johansen to David.

"What would happen if I did approach your navigators station Captain, without clearance?" asked David, while observing the navigator's station, as he stood by the Captain's Chair.

"You would be knocked out by an energy field that maintains a defensive security around the navigator's station. It would be a good hour before you would wake up David and that would be in a secured holding-cell on the Brig Level," replied the captain as he kept an eye on his navigator's station.

In a few minutes they were orbiting an inner planet which is the location of Dr. Carol Marcus's research which is the 'the Goldilox Zone' (a planet orbit around a star in 'the habitable zone', where life has a chance to develop. The 'Goldilox Zone' is where many planetary-mass objects can support liquid water because of satisfactory atmospheric pressure.

"David, we are cleared to beam you down to the staff residential facility. Our transporter system has a biofilter which effectively removes all known viruses whether beaming onto a ship or as we are doing, another location off one's ship. When you and the other three from BathKohl were transported to the Commanders ship you all were automatically scanned, and any new virus was automatically placed into the bio-filter memory. I'm glad to say that no new virus was registered in the scanning between my ship and your Commanders. I just wanted you to know about our bio-filter structure in case anyone asks about virus and germ safety in this process," explained Captain Johansen.

"Captain, do you know if my mother will be in the transporter room when we go down?" asked David as he was watching the planet display on the Command Deck Screen. He was amazed at the size of the dome covering the lab area of his mother's work.

"I have no idea David as I was denied any information in my inquiry as to her whereabouts." I was told I do not have the security clearance for that simple question, but you will be given that clearance after you transport to the lab. After you transport and that confirmation of your safe arrival is immediately received here, then I will return to my mapping studies. My ship will be available for any requests by your mother's lab while we are in this quadrant. I hope to meet your mother as I have wanted to for many years David. Oh, we have an incoming communication from the lab. I'll take that and fill you in on what I hear so just stay here on the bridge David, back in a minute," said Captain Johansen as he walked over to his bridge office.

In a few minutes Captain Johansen returned to Deck Command Chair and informed David that they just got approved to beam down to the Residential Lab of Dr. Carol Marcus. Your mother has not been informed of your arrival David, but I have been informed that immediately upon our arrival we will be escorted to the main lab floor and your mother will be entering shortly. This is just going to be an amazing moment and I'm so glad I'll be there. Are you ready to head to our transporter?" asked the Commander.

"Wow, yes. Thank you, Sir. This is more than I could have dreamed of. And my mother doesn't even know I'm alive, wow. Yes Sir, let's go," replied David with obvious excitement and a few tears on his face, visible to all deck hands, bringing them to the same response. A beautiful, beautiful moment on the Icarus.

David and Captain Johansen transported off the Icarus and arrived in the Residential Lab of Dr. Marcus's team.

"Welcome to "the Regula Terraforming Lab", I am Professor Longin, Chief Assistant to Dr. Carol Marcus. And you must be Captain Johansen, and you're David Marcus, I am correct?"

"You got that right Professor Longin. And may I introduce you to the long thought dead, David Marcus," said Captain Johansen.

"You're both welcome," said Professor Longin as he shook hands with David, and continued saying, "David, you're a miracle, an absolute, unbelievable miracle. As you both requested, I have informed no one as to your arrival and as you can see, I cleared the lab. In a few minutes Dr. Marcus will enter this area from her work of the day. That wall on the other side of this lab from the Transporter Unit is the door to the terraforming work. It is the exit and entrance and directly on the other side of the door are two large sterilizing chambers. That single horn sound you hear right now announces the entry of the staff to the outer Sterilizing Chamber where all clothing is removed to total nudity, and after physical sterilization, the clothing is placed into a replicator.

After the system decides 'all is well on all bodies', the exiting chamber is opened, and sterile clothing is available for all. When the second system decides everyone is clear than what looks like a solid wall will slide open. There will be one more alarm and the doors will open.

I can't wait to see your mothers' response when she returns into this lab and sees you standing at the door. Let's move over to that door David, get you standing right there and then the Captain and I will wait by that desk over there."

A few minutes later David was standing near the door, the second alarm sounded, and the wall door opened as David was physically shaking a little.

Dr. Marcus was looking at some documents as she exited the chamber into the lab and casually looked up and suddenly froze as she looked upon David. David rushed up and grabbed his mother in a big hug. One of the technicians could see Dr. Marcus looking a little weak in her legs so he immediately placed a desk chair behind her. David slowly lowered his mother into the chair, kneeling in front of her, still hugging.

"David, I don't believe it, you're alive, oh my God, David, David," said David's mother as they both held onto each other, swelled in tears.

Another staff member rolled a chair over for David, while everyone moved to the other side of the lab, giving them space to greet each other.

A few minutes later both Professor Longin and Captain Johansen approached the two and stood by them. Professor Longin suggested that David and Dr. Marcus go to the quarters of Dr. Marcus and call the lab for dinner later for anything they might want.

After David and his mother left, Professor Longin introduced the lab staff and Captain Johansen to each other, followed by a walk to the dining hall where conversation went on until late evening.

Everyone planned to meet and talk more at breakfast, around 9 a.m., and no one was to bother Dr. Marcus or David unless called on for any reason.

Breakfast was more like a question-and-answer lecture limited to David's rescue story that Captain Johansen began with the Icarus and its first contact with the unknown Commander LynLouOn of the warship, "Alonfen" ending with the re- union of David Marcus with his mother, Dr. Carol Marcus. Captain Johansen kept all other facts out of his story as he had a commitment to speak only about his meeting with the Alonfen and arriving here with David.

Dr. Marcus and David meet Professor Longin and Captain Johansen in the lab near the doors to the terraforming work of Dr. Marcus.

Captain Johansen approached Dr. Marcus and introduced himself, stating, "Dr. Marcus, I am amazed to be meeting you. I have been following your work for years."

"Thank you Captain and I am honored to meet you. David has told me all about meeting you and being transported to your ship. And about that ship that brought David, "the Alonfen", I should like to hear more of what you might know about that ship and its Commander LynLouOn.

"Ok Dr. Marcus, perhaps this evening we may have time for that. If I might ask Dr. Marcus, why is your work below the surface?" asked Captain Johansen.

Dr. Marcus replied, "it is a testing arena that this is the best mode to test my work. While I won't share anymore on that, but I do have a surprise for you. To express my gratitude for you giving me the unbelievable return of my son, David, I'm taking you both into my work area so you can see my goal in terraforming.

Ok, so first we will enter the outer sterilization chamber where we will strip and hang our clothes, and then each of us will enter what appears to be a shower stall and the system will go through numerous cycles. What appears to be steam will fill the room. Don't worry, it's not a breathing issue.

Then when the chambers clear, the far wall will slide open and we enter the next sterilizing chamber, nude. You leave all possessions you have worn, regardless of what it is, where you have placed them and don't touch your belongings after the sterilizing process. In the second chamber there will be clothing available in a shower stall of the same location of the first chamber.

Ok everyone, I'll open the door and let's go."

After everyone got dressed in the second chamber, Dr. Marcus had everyone stand back from the long blank wall, pressed a button on the right collar of her lab jacket and the wall slid open and then she led them out into a large laboratory.

A few researchers were present and very busy as they did not get up from their stations, only waving at Dr. Marcus and her guests.

"Follow me to my desk and then I will remove the gray from that long wall on the other side of my desk. They all had gathered at the desk of Dr. Marcus, and she said," now I will dial this wall into a clear glass, so give me a minute."

"Soon the wall became clear like a huge picture-window as David gazed in astonishment. There was the largest cavern David had ever seen.

Captain Johansen turned to Dr. Marcus, asking, "Dr., did you create this cavern, I have never seen anything like it."

"No, Captain I did not. I discovered this last year when we were doing a study of surface depth and had the largest echo returns which outlined this cavern. Since then, we have been looking for any type of life form that would, in my opinion, disqualify my terraforming work here. I can say that we have found no life form of any type or size, on the surface or sub-surface. This cavern will be the central location to my terraforming which is only a few months away."

"Mom, this is fantastic. I returned just in time as I have a terraforming formula that I think will stabilize your opening terraforming steps which seems to have been your biggest problem as I understand this right now," said David to his mother as he held both her hands, looking into his mother's beautiful eyes.

"I can't wait for you to lay that out for me David. I don't know how you came up with your formula, but I'll stand by my desk and look at your formula on the wall as you enter it. That wall to our left will display and securely record what you enter from here at my desk. I'll leave you to that right now if that is ok David?" said Dr. Marcus. "No problem, Mom, I'll begin right now," replied David.

While David was entering the formula, Captain Johansen had a short conversation with David's mother and shortly returned to the main lab, beaming back to the Icarus, returning to his assigned mapping duties of this quadrant.

The following day David and his mother began working on placing the formula into the planet terraforming process she had tested numerous times, each attempt failing in planetary stability in a rather short time.

"Mom, I think this formula, added into your process, will bring stability in this accretion process of stable planet formation. What do you think mother?" asked David as he was observing the wall where the computer work was displayed. "Let me study this for a while David," said his mother.

Then Dr. Marcus stood up and made an announcement to her research staff, "Okay everyone, I have here on our computer wall a new formula that David is sharing with us. I am going to read it and I ask all of you to read it and make any notes and on your personal systems, go ahead and enter this and combine it in any way you see workable to my goal of stability. Let's work for two hours and then I will interrupt for any input. If the majority want more time to work in David's formula, then I will order a good meal be set up. We will be doing dinner, back at ya in two hours."

The lab was very active with conversation that was strong but not very loud.

After David entered the formula, his mother let her system do some automatic placement of David's formula with what she and her staff had been working on. The system searched for a working unifying template of the two formulas which took a good hour. Then a good sound effect went off drawing everyone's attention to the board and the resulting formula being displayed.

"Mother, what do you think?" asked David excitedly.

"David, it looks like a stable formula with ongoing stability. David, you amaze me as I have worked for two years on this and what I see here is what I have been searching for all this time. How did you ever manage this, David?" asked Dr. Marcus as she stood, looking in amazement with hands on her hips, at that formula on that wall board.

"I had to do something with all that time I had on BathKohl which was a good two years, right?" said David as he glanced at his mother and then back to looking at the new formula.

"However, you did this David, with some basic checking on the formula, we can call Starfleet Headquarters soon and get an okay to do our first successful terraforming, unless we're missing something in reading this formula, and I don't think we are. Thank you, David!" replied Dr. Marcus.

After three weeks of numerous test runs, the staff of Dr. Marcus, along with herself, concluded they reached the stability they just couldn't get until David added his formula into theirs.

That weekend at the end of that third week, Dr. Marcus threw a large party for her staff, giving a special honor to her son, David. Dr. Marcus stood in front of the screen that displayed the final formula in the labs terraforming work, speaking to her lab, "I want to thank you all for your ongoing patience with me through these two years and especially living with my anger that erupted too many times. And David, returning to me alive and well after two years is the most unbelievable joy-filled event in my life and I express my eternal gratitude to those of the planet BathKohl who rescued you and brought you back to total health, and returning you to me, thank you, thank you.

To my terraforming team the greatest thankyou I can give you is to announce that our Federation has given total approval to our terraforming of this planet. David, I think you will like this, the ship we all will reside on and do our terraforming control from is non-other than 'the Icarus'."

"David, we named the device that will carry our creative compound, "The Genesis Device". Due to your work David, your formula has solved my problem of stability and I believe that at long last we will terraform any life free planet structure into a stable life supporting planet.

I think you'll not only have your degree's again, but Starfleet will want us both at the Academy. As for myself, and hopefully you David, I'm staying in my terraforming, wherever it takes me. David, you have made me the happiest mother in the whole universe!"

CHAPTER 28

AN END CAN BE A BEGINNING

Admiral Richardson was looking out his window, observing through the Golden Gate Bridge a small glint of orange on the horizon, sunrise was on the way. Then he turned around facing Lieutenant Gonzalez on the far side of his desk, with his hand behind him, and said, "Lieutenant, it's getting to be sunrise and I'm usually not the one to ask, 'what now, but Lieutenant, "What Now"?

"Do you have any questions which I might be able to answer, Admiral?"

"Lieutenant, if David had the final solution to terraforming, how did that terraforming loose its cohesion in such a short time and literally explode?" asked the Admiral.

"Admiral, David did not know that the formula he had stolen was only the formative formula. To my understanding, a stabilization formula was secured in a different lab which David knew nothing about. In short, it took both formulas to create a stabilized terraformed planet, and Dr. Marcus never understood there was a hidden problem in her work, especially after combining the formula from David into her unstable formula."

An announcement interrupted their conversation over the Academy Alert System, "Attention to all at the Starfleet Academy, this is your Academy Director with a most important announcement.

In a few minutes a new Ambassador to our Federation will be arriving here to our Academy, landing at Admiral Richardson's landing pad, being formerly welcomed by Admiral Richardson and Lieutenant Gonzalez.

This Ambassadors name is ShaNeenSed and properly spelling and meaning will momentarily be displayed on all announcement boards. You are all ordered to pay strict attention to the visual announcement. The Ambassador has committed to speak English as none of us are fluent in his language. His displayed name is our English translation of his name and title which will be explained with his name.

Thank you, at ease, carry on."

"Lieutenant, that's another surprise. Your hidden is now going public?" asked Admiral Richardson with a frowning look at his Lieutenant.

"That is a surprise to me also Admiral, totally. Admiral, the formal greeting upon his arrival is in our military style, no arms of any type are allowed on the platform," said Lieutenant Gonzalez to his Admiral.

"I have never heard of that before Lieutenant. While carrying a rifle as a formal greeting may seem very old fashioned, it is a very honorable part of our history. Do you have any idea why we are meeting your ambassador in an un-armed formality?" asked Admiral Richardson as he was checking his formal look in his office mirror.

"Admiral, in this case I can say that the formality is in line with the practice of the Ambassador's home planet, BathKohl," said Lieutenant Gonzalez as was taking his turn looking in the office mirror, checking his formal dress uniform, making sure he looked correct.

"Any idea Lieutenant of what his uniform might look like. I'm more than a little curious?" said the Admiral as he was watching his Lieutenant double check his dress uniform.

"Sir, their dress code is quite different. As I understand this situation, the Ambassador will be dressed in a style that we call a dashiki, although his crew will be in more of our style of a formal military uniform. They all are well versed in our English language and more ready for us, thanks to David, then we are of them," replied Lieutenant Gonzalez.

An announcement over the Academy public system stated that the Admirals arrival would be within ten minutes.

"Okay Lieutenant, we are definitely ready. Let's go Lieutenant," said Admiral Richardson.

As the Admiral Richardson and his secretary, Lieutenant Gonzalez were waiting on the Admirals landing pad, the Admiral was looking out West of the Golden Gate Bridge when he noticed a beautiful ship coming into view. "Lieutenant, that is the most extraordinary ship I have ever seen, it is just beautiful. No doubt that has to be our Ambassador ShaNeenSed. Did I say his name correctly Lieutenant?" said the Admiral, with a glance at his Lieutenant.

"Yes, Sir Admiral, you pronounced his name with titles correctly," answered Lieutenant Gonzalez.

"My God, the ship is landing. It is so quit I find it hard to believe. Lieutenant, this may be the end to your story, but it is a beginning into a new unknown," said Admiral Richardson, in formal salute to the ships opening door.